Hope

This book is for anyone who has ever been in hospital and needed a bit of hope.

And to all the teenage girls out there; you're braver than you know and stronger than you think.

Hope

Rhian Ivory

Firefly

First published in 2017
by Firefly Press
25 Gabalfa Road, Llandaff North, Cardiff, CF14 2JJ
www.fireflypress.co.uk

A CIP catalogue record of this book is available from the British Library.

ISBN 9781910080627
ebook ISBN 9781910080634

This book has been published with the support of the Welsh Books Council
and an Arts Council Author Grant

Typeset by Elaine Sharples

Printed and bound by:
opolgraf ▌▐ ▌▌▐
PRINTING HOUSE

"Hope" is the thing with feathers—
That perches in the soul—
And sings the tune without the words—
And never stops – at all—

And sweetest – in the Gale – is heard—
And sore must be the storm—
That could abash the little Bird
That kept so many warm—

I've heard it in the chillest land—
And on the strangest Sea—
Yet – never – in Extremity,
It asked a crumb – of me.

Emily Dickinson

May

I climb up and lean over the ferry rail, looking down into the grim, grey sea. *I've ruined everything.*

'Want a smoke?' someone asks behind me – a he someone. I shut my eyes tight and pray he'll walk away. I smell tobacco, strong but sweet, and try not to breathe in. I keep my eyes closed – if I can't see him he can't see me. But he leans against the railing I'm standing on and it shakes.

'I won't say "It can't be that bad" cos clearly it is, right? Life's shite. Not all the time, just sometimes.' His accent is very strong – Irish.

I open my eyes a little. Snot is dripping onto my top lip.

'Want to talk?' he asks. He's heard me. He's been watching me. But I don't know *what* he's seen or heard.

'Just piss off!'

He takes a final drag and grinds his fag into the deck with his boot. As he pushes away from the railing it

1

shudders violently. My feet slip. He grabs my denim jacket. He holds on so tightly that I can't breathe. When he lets me go, I drop back hard onto the deck. I'm winded.

'Want to tell me what all the shouting and swearing's about?' he says, pulling me up. I try to push him away but I can't stand up straight. I end up leaning against him despite myself; he's warm and smells funny, slightly sweet. Oh, I get it, not quite cigarettes.

'No.' I spit the word out.

No, I don't want to tell this strange boy I've failed my drama college audition. I definitely don't want to tell him why this latest failure is worse than the others. Because of Dad.

When I was twelve, Dad borrowed an old camper van from someone else in the music department and took Mum and me on holiday to Dublin to show me his old haunts – the flat above the newsagents, Grafton Street where he busked, and Abbey Theatre, where he and Mum first met. Dad kept saying we'd go back again, showing me photos of Mum and me playing on St Stephen's Green and one of Mum and Dad in Temple Bar looking worse for wear. Dad was so happy when I told him I was thinking of applying to Dublin. He said they'd buy a camper van and come to see me every school holiday. Mum just rolled her eyes. Maybe she thought the idea of me going to Dublin to study Drama at sixteen was even more delusional than Dad's crazy camper van idea. I was too embarrassed to ask.

2

No one else in our group had thought of Ireland until I told them all about the course there. Even Mr Davis didn't know about it. Dublin's not far from us, just across the water really. When they heard the words 'Young RADA' almost everyone applied, even those who'd already got conditional offers elsewhere, which felt a bit excessive. Maybe I should have kept it to myself. I remember the day I got the letter through with the dates for the second auditions. I was so proud. Mr Davis told us that being recalled for second auditions meant they were taking you seriously. And I believed him, especially about the singing audition. 'No one else will stand a chance when they hear you, Hope,' he said and I trusted him. *Fool.*

'I'll guess then?'

The boy pulls me into an alcove tucked out of the way of the rain. He wraps his leather jacket round my shoulders. It stinks of smoke. I shrug it off. He puts it back. I give up.

'I'm only after keeping you dry and warm. The state of you, you're shaking.'

He lights up another not-cigarette and takes a long drag, flickering it to life. He offers it to me. I take it – I've no idea why – and hold it, letting the heat sear into my skin. I consider throwing it into the sea but don't have the energy. I give it back to him.

'Alright then, let me guess… You've split up with your fella?'

A noise comes out of me, like a snort and a laugh – a snarf. I hope it conveys what an arse I think he is. This has nothing to do with boys. There's no point trying to tell him what it is about because even *I* don't understand.

'Ah, hang on, you've not run away from home, have you? Seriously? *Shite!*' He leans forward, looking properly worried, taking in my damp clothes and messy hair. He looks around as if expecting to see the police or something. 'C'mon now, out with it, are you after running away?'

I shake my head but he won't stop staring at me with that look, concern for the crazy girl, and I don't want to see it anymore. I try to glance inside through the steamy windows, but my glasses are messed up. I pull my t-shirt out from under my other layers and wipe them clean. With them back on, I can just make out the shapes of the navy-blue headrests. My friends are in there with my teacher, laughing, drinking and celebrating. I should be in there, with Callie and my friends, instead of out here with this random boy.

'Ah, here, sorry. I didn't mean to be a dick. I was just trying to distract you, to cheer you up like.' He finishes his joint and flicks it away from us. The wind sends it rolling over the deck and into the sea. 'Lookit, I'm Riley. Riley Santiago. I wasn't stalking you, I'm scarlet you'd think that. I only came out here for a cheeky smoke but then I heard you wailing and whining and I could hardly walk away?'

He turns me round slowly, gently. I take him in, this

4

Riley Santiago. His eyes are brown and hooded under heavy lids. His lips are thick and bouncy looking, like a ripe peach. His skin is dark, rich with beauty spots and moles chucked across his nose and cheeks, as if someone has decorated him with paint but he's been too busy to clean it off. He looks like the kind of boy who should come with a warning, just to give you a fighting chance.

'I'm fine,' I lie, as I shrug off his jacket.

'Is there someone I can get for you? Who are you on the ferry with?' He looks around, past me into the restaurant.

'*No! No!* I don't need anyone!'

The last thing I need is him finding Mr Davis or Callie. I don't want them to see me like this.

'Alright, well, if you won't let me get someone then I want your phone number.'

He holds out his hand.

I ignore him.

He walks to the door with a threatening look on his face.

I reach into my jacket pocket and pull out my phone. He comes back over to me and takes it.

'I'm going to put my number in your phone and I want you to call me, or text, whatever. That's the deal. I can't just let you go, the state you're in.'

Even though he's sort of making a joke there's something serious there, and it's nice. He means well, I think, but what would I know? I wonder if I can grab my phone back and bolt.

He stays far too close to me, taking his sweet time typing in numbers and letters. He smiles as he puts my phone back in my top pocket, before pulling me back into him by the edges of my jacket. I don't move away. He's deciding what to do next. I'm trying to second-guess what he'll do. I wait for the words.

'I won't go in there and find your parents or whatever – you nearly died when I suggested that – but I want a text from you later to say *I'm alive* or I can't let you go, and we'll be stuck together forever like this. Is that what you want?'

He locks both his arms tightly around my back and smiles at me again and, for a stupid second, I think he's going to kiss me. It makes me feel nervous.

'Okay! Whatever it takes to get rid of you. I was fine until you came along!' I push him away.

He laughs as if this is funny. But he does let go of me.

He zips the neck of his jacket up and pats me on the shoulder in a matey way and the tension is broken, the almost-moment evaporates. He takes a melodramatic comedy step away from me and then starts talking again.

'Now, I won't lie and promise it's all going to be fine. But I have a feeling about you, a wee feeling but a good one, *nameless girl*.' He opens the door, lifting his feet carefully so he doesn't trip.

'Hope!' I shout, just before the door closes. 'My name's Hope,' I add, in case he thinks I'm just shouting words at him.

He raises his hand, to say goodbye – or *I heard*, or *Whatever* – and walks into the steamy restaurant. The ferry sounds its loud horn as it approaches the docks. Home.

The journey home to Shrewsbury from Holyhead in the minibus with Mr Davis and the rest of them is torture. My face says it all when Mum finally turns up. Her *sorry* falls flat onto the pavement and I don't have the heart to hug her back as she wraps her arms around me. I just hang there, limp, letting her *never mind* slide off me like the rain.

I see the concentration scratched across her face as she drives out of the car park. An oncoming lorry honks at her and she mutters something then catches my eye. She searches for something to say to break the stale layers of silence in the car, then turns the radio up.

I know she thinks I'm a failure, even though she won't say it. She'd told everyone at work: I know because I saw it all over Facebook one night when she'd left her page open on her mobile. 'So proud of my girl being recalled to audition in Dublin, knew she'd get through to the 2nd stage for Young RADA!'

And other status updates with more smiley faces. I didn't want her putting my news on Facebook, but at the same time it made me feel good that she was proud of me. Now what does she have to be proud of?

'So how did Callie and Aisha get on? Sounds tough. Did you know some drama schools accept less than one per cent of the applicants,' Mum tells me, sounding like she's swallowed a prospectus, or she's been reading *How to Talk to Your Teen*. I appreciate the effort, I really do, but I want her to stop trying to make things better. I know she's building up to asking me what went wrong. But I can't tell her or Mr Davis or even Callie. Because I can't remember.

'Niall got through to the workshop day. Aisha didn't get in either but she's got a conditional offer from Liverpool Sixth Form at LIPA which is great,' I choke out, not meaning a single word. 'Callie was rejected but she's probably going to get a call-back from the Birmingham Theatre School.' I hear the sourness in my voice. Niall now has offers from Young Actors' Studio at the Royal Welsh College of Music and Drama and Italia Conti. He'll probably get Young RADA too, he's spoilt for choice.

'I'm sorry, I know how much you wanted this.' She accelerates as if getting me home is the answer. I bet the first thing she does when we get in is offer me a cup of tea or suggest I take Scout out for a walk to clear my head.

'Thanks, Mum.' I close my eyes and hope she gets the message. I lean back against the headrest, picturing the twists and turns in the road as we get closer to home. The last place I want to be.

'Hope, I'm taking Scout for a walk… Want to come?' Mum calls up to me.

I ignore her. I fling my bag on my bed, shut the door and sit on the floor.

'Hope? I'm going then.'

I wait until I hear the back door click shut then I get back up again. I don't know what to do with myself. I don't want to be here, in my room, but I don't know where to go either. I prowl my bedroom, but there isn't much space so I put some music on. I lie on my bed and notice my poster of *Macbeth* with Judi Dench as Lady M is peeling off the wall a bit. I try to stick it back but the Blu-tack's gone dry. I don't want Dame Judi to look at me the way she is – judging me. So I rip it right off the wall, bunching it up in my hand so that the edges cut my skin. I rip up the prospectus for Young RADA, which is difficult. I can't tolerate the smiling student faces shining out from every page. I tear down every photo from the pinboard: me playing Meg Long from *Our Country's Good* and Shen Te in *The Good Person of Szechwan*. I rip up the picture of me in my favourite role as Christina in *Dancing at Lughnasa* and shove them all into my new wastepaper bin, letting the pins stab my hand. The bin is too full. I shove and squeeze and then I hit it. I hit the bin with the palm of my hand.

I hit it with my fist.

I kick it.

I hit it again. Hard.

It shatters down the middle like it has been struck by lightning.

I feel shame in my stomach. I've smashed the lid of my brand new bin and there's a massive crack running down the side of it. I try to push the edges back together so the damage isn't quite so obvious but it doesn't work. I know I hit it, but it didn't feel that hard, not enough to split it in two. I couldn't have broken it so easily, could I?

Time passes; I don't know how much. I sit on the floor panting, looking around at the mess I've made. My clothes have been flung with force from my overnight bag. My desk chair is upended, the wheels spinning uselessly, and one of my snow globes has smashed, leaving a little pool on my desk, shards of glass swimming in the remains.

I think there's something wrong with me.

Before we left for Dublin I made an arrogant promise to Mum that if I didn't make this audition I'd give up on trying to get into drama college. Mum worked out that she'd spent almost £60 on each audition, plus the travel costs to get there and back, the youth hostel we stayed in for Dublin, the B&B in Cardiff and the others, *all* the others. She'd agreed to let me apply for five drama colleges and no more. I went for it thinking I wouldn't need more than three but better to be safe than sorry: Liverpool, Cardiff, London, Manchester and then the fifth and final audition in Dublin.

But I only said it because I never thought I'd fail. Up till now it's all come so easy. I've had all the parts I've wanted. I've had it all planned out since I was little – pantomimes, concerts, youth opera group, school plays, drama club, youth theatre, singing in the chorus for touring musicals, stage school in the summer holidays when Mum and Dad could afford it, GCSE Drama and then drama college before auditioning for drama school. What am I supposed to do now? Mum keeps talking about Plan B but Plan Bs are for people who fail.

I just never,

not once,

not even for a tiny moment, thought that I would need one.

'Hope! Are you coming to eat your tea or not? Scout's eyeing it up!' Mum shouts over my music. I hear the oven door slamming, the clattering of cutlery and an impatient bark from Scout, always on the lookout for food. I switch my music off, reply to another text from Callie, reassuring her that I'm fine. No one who says 'I'm fine!' really means it and Callie and I both know this. I shove my phone in my back pocket and go downstairs.

I sit at the table while Mum remains standing. I forgot she was out tonight. I look down at my plate. Jacket potato and beans is cop-out cooking. There's a cup of tea going cold next to my plate. I can't stand cold tea but I sip it so as not to hurt her feelings. She didn't have to cook for me tonight, not when it's book-club night. 'Thanks, Mum, this looks great.' I try to sound like I mean it.

'It's pay day tomorrow. We could get some nice food

for the weekend, maybe even a meal deal? And we could go into town. I'd like to get you some new clothes for starting work, until we can get your top ordered in. I'm sure there's a few sales on. New start next month, once you've finished your exams,' she chatters, gathering up her car keys with a smile as she heads to the back door.

'Don't remind me,' I mutter.

She stops near the door. I watch her shoulders rise with tension and then drop with an effort. I know she's trying, but I can't meet her halfway, not tonight.

'Hope, we've talked about this. You agreed. I *know* you don't want to spend the summer with me at work but we made a deal.'

I don't want to work with her. I want to stay here in the house on my own and just…

'You are not going to waste the summer hanging around the house! Moping about won't make anything better.' She comes back to the table and pulls out a chair. 'It'll just make you feel worse, trust me.'

I want her to go and take her well-meant assumptions about my feelings with her. She's doing her 'I'm your parent not your best friend' thing and tonight it's making my skin crawl. She thinks I can just work through the summer and go to Shrewsbury Sixth-Form College, as if that's all I've ever dreamed of.

'You're not the only one, are you? Callie and Aisha didn't get in either. I guess the timing doesn't help?' She pauses.

'You're probably feeling worse about it all because you're hormonal at the moment.'

Hormonal is the understatement of the year. I'm getting angrier each month, more aggressive and less in control. And it's scaring me, really scaring me. Sometimes I've not been able to keep it in, even at school. I can hear what I'm saying, can imagine my face contorting as the spiteful words come out of my mouth and I don't want to be like this. I don't want to be constantly apologising for whatever's just come out of my mouth.

I tried managing myself with fake days off each month, but Mum cottoned on and forced me out of bed. It isn't that my periods are that painful. Then I'd take some tablets, grab a hot water bottle and eat some chocolate, just like the other girls do. But my mood swings are not like everyone else's.

'We can talk about things when I get back from the Bird's Nest book club. Or come with me, if you want?' She puts her copy of the new Kate Atkinson on the table as an offering.

'I'll be fine. I've got loads of stuff to do. You *go!*' I pull up the corners of my mouth with force, even though I know my eyes won't match. 'Have a good time!'

She nods at my fake smile, kisses the top of my head and rushes out. Her long hair smells of coconut and I just manage to stop myself grabbing hold of it and wrapping it around my neck like a noose so that she can't leave me.

15

I don't want to scare her with this, I'm not ready. Neither of us are.

I listen to the house once she's gone. Scout barks at someone daring to walk past, something clangs in the washing machine, there's a whirring or a pulse coming from the walls as if the house is alive, breathing, waiting for my next move.

I don't know what to do once I've eaten. I can't even think about revising, there's no way any of it would go in. I stupidly presumed we'd be out celebrating. I slump over to the sofa. I don't reach for the TV remote. I don't glance at the shiny magazines Mum's brought home from work. I just sit and feel blank. Scout gives me the eye but I don't feel like taking her for a walk right now. She's far too happy and bouncy. I close my eyes and fall into a sleep that's filled with falling off cliffs and tripping over curbs.

The text makes me jump. It vibrates in the back pocket of my jeans, insistent. It's probably Callie, she's not going to give up tonight. It might be easier to go out with her.

It vibrates again. I shove my glasses up my nose as the third text announces its arrival. I swipe the screen to unlock it. It's not Callie. It's him – him from the ferry, him – Riley Santiago.

How r y? Grand?

Come on now, you know the deal, you're supposed to tell me you're alright so I don't have to alert the guards!

Checked your email lately? Got your attention now haven't I! ;)

What does he mean check my email? He hasn't got my email address.

I fling my phone onto the sofa. Scout barks at me in excitement as I run upstairs. My laptop hums into life when I open it. The screen says it is starting 1 of 3 updates and not to shut it down. I run back downstairs to read his texts again, trying to decode them. Scout paces back and forth, looking hopefully at the back door. Has Riley sent me an email? Has he hacked my email? Does he know something I don't?

Maybe… Maybe I've got a second chance, another audition? But how could he know that, unless he was at Dublin, too? He looked like an actor; his name is definitely showy enough, unlike mine, Hope Baldi.

'Riley Santiago.' I try the sound of his name out loud. Definitely an actor. I bet he has an Equity card. He could be a talent scout! Maybe he saw something in me? Maybe he was at the audition and disagreed with the others? It happens, you hear about it all the time. *All the time.*

I run back up the stairs. My homepage is loading. I click on the envelope icon and wait. I have one new mail. I hit the key and it opens.

Just checking in to make sure you aren't scaring any more gulls with your screeching, banshee girl. Car's got a flat battery. Telly's shite. What r u doing?

So no. He isn't anyone. He doesn't have anything to tell me. He's talking about telly and cars and he can't even type. He's doing text talk on his email as if these are interchangeable. How did he get my email? I fire back frustration and disappointment:

Stalker! How did you get my email?

There's no reply. I click the refresh button. Nothing. I thought he said he was bored.

I put some music on to drown out my own voice. I go to the bathroom and check the spots on my forehead as a distraction – it doesn't work. I come back and there's an email sat there waiting. I ought to delete it but I can't.

Sent myself an email from yr phone on the ferry. Insurance policy in case you ignored my texts. And guess what... you did. Want to skype?

He's clearly a flake. He thinks we have some kind of connection. He thinks we're what... *friends*? Skype? He sounds at least three beers into his evening. I'm not skyping him. I've got to shut this down before it gets out of hand. I need to get rid of him.

No, I don't want to Skype – don't even know you. Delete me from your phone.

I wait for his reply but there's no response.

July

'Hope, I've asked Owen and Pryia to look after you today. You can shadow them this week and then you can shadow me and Nikhil the week after?' I'm the only trainee this summer, and despite my induction I'm nervous. Mum runs through her staff list as if I should know them. The last time – I can't think about the last time I saw them – the last time I refused to look at them and pretended that I couldn't hear their sympathetic words and sorries when they came back to the house afterwards. And now I'm in a place I vowed I'd never return to – a hospital. Trapped here for the whole summer.

The automatic doors magically open as we approach. Dad's joke about using the force to part the doors plays like an old black and white film in my head. I run up the ramp after Mum, leaving the memory behind me, and I'm hit by the stench of clinical cleanliness.

'Morning, Erin. Hey, Hope.' It's Nikhil, Mum's partner at

work. I feel embarrassed. He'll know all about my auditions. But he doesn't even say 'Sorry' or 'Things will work out.'

As Mum fills out some paperwork at reception, Nikhil rubs his hands under a cleaning gel dispenser, gesturing that I should do the same. My skin absorbs the gel in seconds but I keep rubbing my hands for something to do while we stand by the lift waiting, him smiling and smelling nice, and me breathing in and out, trying not to sweat with nerves.

In case anyone doesn't know who Nikhil is, the massive capital letters SINGING MEDICINE TEAM on the back of his purple polo shirt should make it clear. Nikhil's clean looking, like his whole body has just come out of the washing machine. His top is crisp and smells freshly ironed. As we get out of the lift, Mum is coming up from the stairwell. She never uses the lift unless she's with a patient, says the stairs are healthier. She and Nikhil fall into step and I follow along a corridor inventively called Hospital Street.

When we get to the staffroom, I sit next to the kettle and fiddle with the milk, feeling out of place. I watch them rushing about, gathering up purple buckets full of musical instruments, ward sheets hidden in purple plastic wallets and bottles of hand-sanitising gel. They don't look like nurses and doctors but there's an air of medicine about them, a smell of something clean and smart about their purple Singing Medicine polo shirts.

'Come on then, Hope. Come and meet the children on Pan ward!' Pryia says, holding open the door to a corridor full of posters, paintings and photos of smiling children. I can't help but notice her belt. It has the Catwoman symbol on it. She sees me checking it out, grins, then passes me a name badge. I reluctantly stick it onto my new shirt, pricking my finger on the pin. Pryia passes me a Gruffalo plaster. She clicks her tongue at me as if to say to take more care.

There's a big sign saying RENAL outside the Peter Pan ward, which is noisy with footsteps, trolley wheels rolling, curtain rails being pulled back, spoons clattering against bowls and chatter everywhere. The patients are having their breakfast. This must be a high point in the day as the children seem a bit hyper. As I walk down the ward the noise grows. Owen is waving to the children, laughing at some of the things they say as he bounces past them. His trainers squeak on the floor like manic mice. The children's noise is because of them – Pryia and Owen. The kids sit up looking hopeful. Some of them were watching individual TV screens pulled down over their beds but now their attention is firmly fixed on the Singing Medicine team. It's like a celebrity has walked into the room.

Each kid is hooked up to a machine which whirrs and clicks. A dial spins around constantly and I see red coming out of one of the tubes.

'They're having dialysis, the machine is cleaning their

blood. They have to sit still for up to four hours. See that there? That's a Hemo-Cath, which is basically their lifeline, so they can't jump around too much,' Pryia tells me. They've got tubes going into their noses as well. I'm not sure what they do – could be food or oxygen, I guess. Most have a parent holding their hand, or watching the telly with them. One parent and a little girl are doing some colouring-in, but she stops to look up when she hears Owen's footsteps. Her face changes, excitement making her sit up.

'*OWEN!*' shouts a small boy with a big afro. He breaks into a smile as Owen pulls a silly face at him and shakes a maraca. Then Owen and Pryia start singing and everything changes.

It isn't just the atmosphere on the ward. It's more than that. The air fills with something. Even the nurses change the way they walk: they are smoother and almost fade into the background. The singing has a soothing effect like a salve and envelops everyone in its magic.

In the corner I spot a girl who looks much older than the others, and is almost tucked away from them behind a partition. No one sits with her. She doesn't move as I walk up to her bed so I whisper, 'Are you awake?'

She doesn't reply.

'She's awake.' A nurse appears from nowhere. I've got no idea what to do as he checks her blood pressure. I look at the big machine she's hooked up to. It says Gambro on the front and is bluey green. I try not to look at her blood – it seems way too personal, but I can't help it. I watch her blood coming out of her body and going into the machine, which turns constantly and makes a strange sound. I wonder if you get used to it. The nurse makes notes on a clipboard at the end of the girl's bed. I feel in the way and lean over to make sure he can get past me. I don't know where to put myself.

The girl doesn't register me, as if she's pretending she's not in the room with us. She looks about twelve. Her hair is tucked away under a sky-blue hijab with tiny silver stars on it. I sit on the chair near the little cupboard on wheels next to her bed. I try and make myself small and let them get on with it, but the nurse shakes his head at me.

'Aren't you going to sing to her?' He's obviously used to the Singing Medicine team.

'Um, no,' I tell him, hoping he'll leave me be. He stands there, looking pointedly at my name badge. I get his confusion. I'm confused too. How the hell am I going to make it through this summer in a team of singers when I can't trust my voice anymore?

'Well, make yourself useful then.' He passes me a hot-pink book with yellow writing on the cover, holding it across the girl's bed until I have to take it. I wait for further instruction but he walks off. He's left me on my own with her, as if I know what I'm doing. I turn the book over in my hands and read the blurb on the back.

Sunny, Kitty and Hannah are set for the Best. Summer. Ever.

Of course they are, everyone's going to have a ball this summer. I open the book to a creased-down page. I look around in search of inspiration but everyone is doing something. There's no way I'm going to ask for help so soon. I can do this. I'm not totally useless. I tap her very gently on the shoulder and hold the book out to her, hoping she might take it, but she blanks me. I start reading aloud.

The sign above the Harry Potter ward says Burns Unit. Owen and Pryia pause outside a small room before the doors to the main ward and I stop, wondering why we're not going through. Owen squirts some gel from the bottle clipped onto his belt, rubs it over his hands and waits for Pryia to do the same. There's yellow and black tape around the floor, as if the room has been cordoned off like a crime scene. The sign says Protective Isolation. Pryia follows Owen in, but holds the edge of the door so firmly, I almost crash into her.

'Ah, I'd forgotten you wouldn't be able to come in here with us. We'll catch up with you in about ten minutes, okay?' Behind her I see Owen put on a mask, apron and gloves, before she sharply pushes the door shut.

'Where do they all come from, the patients?' I ask Owen, when they come out of the small room ten minutes later.

'Birmingham mostly and the rest of the Midlands, but we get people coming from further afield, especially north Wales. This is one of the best children's hospitals in the UK,' he answers, with pride in his voice. Owen is a nurse here as well as working with Singing Medicine. 'Come on, we're going to go onto the main burns ward now. If you need to get out you hit the green button and this is the code. I've written it down for you. Have you ever been on a burns ward before?'

I shake my head.

'If you feel uncomfortable, that's understandable, but you mustn't make the patients feel uncomfortable. Say you've got to go to the toilet or need to make a phone call, then leave quietly and we'll find you when we're done.' He obviously thinks I'm not going to be able to cope. How bad is this going to be? Mum wouldn't let me see anything really traumatic, would she?

I follow Owen and Pryia, who stop in front of bright red, yellow and blue sofas that look very Ikea. A pair of crutches are propped up against one. Pryia and Owen hand out instruments and wait patiently for the kids to settle down. Parents stand awkwardly behind them, looking as if they'd rather be somewhere else. I keep my eyes on the parents for a second before forcing myself to look at the children. I tell myself not to stare at them but it doesn't matter because they're all busy staring at me. They whisper behind their hands but Pryia is on to them.

26

'Yeah, yeah, a new person. Now hush it!' she joked, grinning. 'This is Hope. She's going to be joining us for a bit. And I know you'll make her feel welcome.'

Owen winks at me and starts singing, just like that, with no introduction. He's bordering on cheesy, but all the kids join in. I don't know the song. I shake my tambourine, pretending that I'm fine with all of this singing, smiling and generally being super happy, even though one girl's hands are so burned that she can't hold an instrument. She's bandaged up to both her elbows and holds them away from her body at an awkward angle. Her eyes look squashed as if her skin has swollen up. But she's laughing and singing and asking Owen to use rude words. Her dad rolls his eyes at her toilet humour and goes back to texting. I stop second-guessing what's happened to these children. But I don't sing because I can't, nothing comes out when I try. It's like that part of my voice box has been switched off and I've no idea why. I'd fake it if I could or even hum at least, but singing isn't something you can fake, unlike my smile.

They sing three songs, not nursery rhymes and not hymns either. They sing funny counting songs with animal sounds, then they switch and sing personal songs they must have written about healing. I didn't realise they wrote their own songs. I mean, Mum must have mentioned it, but I didn't take it in properly. I thought they just altered ones from a song book or something like that. They sing stories and when they use one of the kid's names in the song you can tell who Becky, Max or Raja is because they sit up taller and don't take their eyes off Owen or Pryia. The singing casts a spell over all the children, taking them somewhere else. I play a triangle, ambitiously moving on from the tambourine. Pryia looks at me when I don't join in with the singing, but she doesn't ask me why and I'm relieved. When they finish, the kids are calmer – it's like a musical form of medicine, a bit like magic, except I'm too old to believe in that anymore.

'How are you doing, Hope?' Owen asks, steering me towards a row of blue chairs lined up against the wall. We sit down and he rubs his hands over his face, his stubble making a scratching sound like sandpaper.

'Fine,' I lie. 'How come I couldn't go in that isolation room with you?' I can't help asking.

He pauses to search for the right answer.

'Doesn't matter. Don't worry if you can't tell me. I shouldn't have asked.' I'm not a member of the team so there's obviously stuff they can't tell me. And that's completely fine.

'The patient has only just been moved from HDU. The patient is now in isolation, so that complicates things a little.'

'What's HDU?' I feel like I should already know. I wish he'd stop saying 'the patient'.

'High Dependency Unit. It isn't quite as critical as an

ICU – you know Intensive Care – it's more of an intermediate measure before going back to the main ward,' he explains, tucking the bottom of his polo shirt into the top of his trousers. I delete ICU from my mind before it can pin me to the floor and stop me breathing. I have to change the subject.

'What about that girl on the renal ward, Pan Ward? The older one, what's the matter with her?' I gulp in air and force out the question.

'Fatima? She's here on dialysis, but now she desperately needs a kidney transplant. She's been waiting a long time for a donor match.'

'Long waiting list?'

'It isn't just that, it's more about the patient's ethnicity. About twenty-five per cent of the organ donor waiting list is made up of black or ethnic minority patients but only eight per cent of the population are black or from ethnic minority groups and not everyone wants to be a donor,' he explains, adding, 'she's got the best chance here in Birmingham but we just don't know how long she could be waiting. Not all faiths believe in organ donation. That can mean we have fewer kidneys for girls like Fatima.'

'I knew there was a shortage of donors but I didn't realise it had anything to do with religion.'

'Well, now you know.' He gets to his feet. I don't know what to say so I get up too and follow him and Pryia down the corridor.

6

At lunchtime I check my phone because it makes me look busy. There's another text from Callie about meeting up. I hover my fingers over the screen, wondering which excuse to roll out this time, as my phone buzzes in another text. I almost say his name out loud in disbelief. I don't know if I'm supposed to feel cross, stalked or something else. Mum has picked a table right in front of the specials board in Joe's Café. I order pumpkin soup with pecan and honey bread then open the text, turning away from Mum. I don't need to worry, she's knee deep in conversation with Nikhil about this year's big charity concert.

How r u? I'm grand thanks for asking. Wait, you didn't ask. Rude!

Is that it? Why bother sending such a tragic text? I put the phone down on the table and sip my Diet Coke. I eavesdrop on four different conversations but can't settle on any of them. I take my glasses off and wipe underneath my eyes, checking my finger for mascara. My soup's arrived but it's too hot to eat. I pick up the phone and I text back.

Bet your name isn't even Riley Santiago. I've tried to find you. You don't exist. Or you've given me a fake name.

I press send before I can stop myself and turn my phone over. Mum finishes her conversation with Nikhil and turns to me.

'How is it going?' She looks anxious. 'You look tired. You're not worrying about your exam results, are you?' Before I can think of an answer she carries on. 'I know it must feel like you've got so much to think about at the moment, but just try to enjoy the summer?'

I nod and smile and pretend that I can just switch off. What if I fail all my GCSEs? Or don't pass enough to get into Shrewsbury College? If I can't do drama, what'll I study? What if I fail A levels too, and can't get on a good university course, and can't get a decent job to pay off all the student loans I'm going to have to take out? Will I still be living with Mum when I'm thirty because I can't afford a mortgage?

As if she senses this swirl terrorising my head, she puts her hot hand on my cheek. She smells of coconut and something else, something chemical. She's poised to offer more advice when Pryia taps her on the arm to ask about a hospital in Oxford.

I look around the room. Everyone is talking to someone,

31

reading or doing something on a phone. I turn my phone over.

I am wounded. Mortally wounded that you'd think I'd make up a fake name. I've no time for social media shite like Shitchat, Instagrime, FakeBook or Twatter so there's no point in trying to stalk me.

I'm not the stalker here!

Talking of fake names I've decided that your name isn't really Hope. It's a joke isn't it?

So you did hear me then? If you think my name's a joke let's not even start on my surname.

Ah here, you have to tell me now!

Nope. Not a chance.

Alright then, what would you change your name to if you could?

A name that doesn't have another meaning like mine does. What about you?

If it ain't broke don't fix it sweetheart. Seriously now, I've already got a deadly name.

I'd like to change my age too. I'd love to fast forward and not be sixteen.

Ah, shite. Are you only 16? You look at least 18.

Of course I look older, that's the whole point isn't it.

Sounds sexy, tell me more Mature Martha.

I wouldn't pick Martha.

What's wrong with Martha? I used to know a grand girl called Martha...

Ugh! Way too early in the morning to hear about you and your back catalogue.

Calm down Cassie. And I don't exactly keep a catalogue ;)

Cassie's nice, that might work.

And where would you go, what would you do as this Cassie one?

I dunno. Maybe go somewhere like Africa and help build a school or do something that might actually make a real difference.

One life live it! Sorry, me Da has Land Rover slogans all over the place.

But I don't have the money to take a gap year and travel.

Get a job. That's my grand plan. Earn some euros and get out of here.

I've already got a job.

Then stop your whingeing Wendy and start saving.

I wouldn't pick Wendy, she does herself no favours massaging Peter Pan's tender little ego.

Er... maybe we didn't watch the same Disney cartoon? I would have definitely remembered Wendy giving Peter a massage. For the record I prefer your version.

Disappointing, *Dublin*, deeply disappointing. So, moving on, are you off to Thailand or Australia, Mr Cliché?

Lucky guess Lorna, I'm going to both! Come with me it'll be a gas.

I don't know what to text back, so I wait for him to say more but that's it, he's gone, and I'm left wondering if he means it.

7

Mum pulls onto the dual carriageway and puts her foot down, heading for the motorway junction, as I prise off my new heels and rub my sweaty feet. Trainers next week, I decide, before registering that there'll be a next week, that I'll be coming back. I still don't have a plan B; nothing has miraculously pinged into my inbox. Must be too full of rejection emails.

When we get home, Mum does her usual Friday-night routine which I've never really understood before, but now I get. She has a long shower without any music. She calls it her wind down and I've always thought it was a bit melodramatic but now I understand. The house is silent, there's no TV on, not even the kettle boiling like a rocket ship ready to launch, yet all I can hear is chatter, screaming, singing, laughing and crying. I can hear the wheels of the nurse's trollies going up and down the echoey hallways. Pens clicking, scratching across charts which clang as they are clipped back on the ends of metal bed frames. Shoes squeaking across the ward. I can smell disinfectant and something else, a sweet smell that is almost sickly, that hospital smell that's indescribable but you know it when you smell it. It makes me think of fear.

I wait for Mum to get out of the shower, wishing we had more than one. When I get in, I turn the water on full blast and just stand there, letting it pummel down on my head, in my eyes, over my shoulders. I stay in there until the water isn't hot anymore.

Later, after we've finished the reheated chilli, Mum puts the TV on and I sit next to her on the sofa, restless. The leather sticks against my leg, making a slurping noise.

'There's a Jane Austen on, want to watch it with me?' Mum asks. I shake my head. 'But you loved *Pride and Prejudice…*' She looks confused.

'That was last year, Mum. I'm not into costume dramas anymore.'

'Come on, give it the ten-minute test? This one's called *Sense and Sensibility.*' She moves up the sofa for me.

'Ten minutes. But if someone falls in love at first sight I'm out of here,' I warn.

She offers me a bar of chocolate. I put my feet up on her lap and make a space by my hip for Scout. Mum pretends to frown but she's even softer than I am on the dog. Within five minutes Scout is lying on top of me and snoring, her velvet spaniel ears drooping over my thigh.

After the film has finished, and Marianne has *finally* worked out that the Alan Rickman character was THE ONE all along, not instalove Willoughby, I prise myself away from Mum and Scout and go up to my room. I drop down onto my desk chair. I am wide awake, it's only nine o'clock. I could read a book, sort out my room or do a witch hazel face mask. Instead, before I've really thought it through, I open my inbox and scroll through my emails. Another boring one from Spotify and some junk mail. I check my spam folder, I even check my trash can. Nothing.

I close my laptop, not allowing myself to click the Facebook icon or the little blue bird. As a delaying tactic I clean my glasses before unlocking my mobile, lying back on my bed. I press on the envelope and see a shiny new email flashing provocatively at me. I tell myself to ignore it and not be so weak, so needy and well … desperate. Then I open it.

Dear Miss Baldi, thank you for attending the Young RADA audition day in Dublin. Unfortunately you didn't…

I don't read any more, I just can't. I press the delete button down hard and hold it until my finger starts to go purpley blue. I knew there'd be a letter, something official on nice paper, but I hadn't thought they'd email me too. How many more ways can they tell me?

I keep thinking if I can just forget it then I'll be able to move on or get past it. I've been getting used to forgetting stuff lately, but I don't seem to have any control over which information my brain chooses to hold on to. And for some reason this particular scene has been deleted and I'm left standing on an empty stage with all the lights out.

On Tuesday morning Mum gets another letter from the bank. I hate seeing the symbol on the front. I shove them down the side of the microwave or in the recycling bin, so she doesn't have to see them. The letters used to come for Mr and Mrs Baldi but now they're just for her. At first it was brutal to see his name dropping through the letterbox in the mornings, as if nothing had happened. But now I miss seeing his name on letters and even the junk mail. I miss seeing his name. To the bank it is as if he doesn't even exist anymore. There's only one place left I could see his name now and I can't go there because Mum isn't talking to Nonno, after the huge argument they had about organ donation. Dad is buried in the Baldi family plot in Italy and we are left here without him.

I can't think about the different parts of him she gave away, the organs that might be inside someone else right now, making them breathe and walk around when he cannot. I don't know what I feel about it. His heart stopped working so surely the rest of him would too? I left ICU each time Mum and Nonno started arguing – I couldn't bear to listen to them discuss Dad like he was just a list of body parts. And because of that I didn't get to say goodbye.

The letters were yellow and full of cells and light. I can see the sign for ICU as if it is in front of me again. I am sitting on that blue chair waiting outside Dad's room and all I can see is the sign – ICU. I read it until the symbols lose all meaning. The letters look like another language someone has made up. I can't interpret it or understand. I am not in the room with them because they are arguing, again. I can't go back with Mum and Nonno and hear them discuss what to do if, what will happen if, what if he doesn't… Someone asks me something, someone in uniform. No sound comes out of my throat. I am mute. Voiceless. Soundlessly I ignore them and hope they'll go away. I hope they'll do the right thing and just leave me be, sat outside ICU on my own.

I read the sign again, it's still there, bright yellow in my eyes, but then there's more than one of them, there's two, then three, then six or seven in uniform appearing from different directions. They're running past me, they're shouting words in their alien hospital code and someone is pushing a cart with equipment on it and Dad's door is swung open. Then Dad's door closes and I stand outside it. I want to ask someone for help. I want to call out to one of the running people to come and help me open the door because I've forgotten how to make it work. My hand is shaking so badly and I've forgotten how to do the handle. I am on the outside looking in and the noises coming from his room are loud and frightening, filling my ears so that I can't even hear my own voice anymore or any of the thoughts in my head. There's no running commentary or internal monologue at all, there's just silence.

And then a beeping replaces the silence.

The beeping penetrates and establishes a rhythm that I move to, swaying back and forth in front of his door like a pendulum. I read the sign again: Intensive Care Unit.

Beeping. Yellow.

I read it over and over.

Yellow. Beeping.

And then the beeping stops.

There is silence inside and outside of me.

And when I sit back down on the blue chair the yellow of the light goes out.

I watch Mum as she slips her shoes on in the hallway, her long auburn hair pulled up into a sharp bun this morning. She looks very serious.

'What's wrong?'

'It's a letter from the bank. Another letter about your dad's estate,' she adds, the word sounding awkward.

'Estate?' I want to laugh, but it's not funny. 'He was hardly Lord of the Manor, more like the groundsman.' I try humour, but it fails.

'It's a bank term, it doesn't mean… Oh, don't worry.' She folds the letter back up. But I do worry.

'Is everything alright?'

She looks at me as if she's about to say something but then changes her mind.

'With the bank, I mean. Is everything okay?'

'There was some paperwork I should have returned, they say that I've missed a date. I need to find his death certificate again.' The words are too heavy for her to hold in her mouth. She's crying. I gently take the envelope from her and hide it behind my back.

'I thought I was keeping on top of things, all this legal paperwork and…' She stops, like she's lost track and then looks at me. 'Did you see any letters they sent?'

I think about all the letters I stuffed into a drawer, or down the side of the microwave and the ones that I recycled.

'Um, not really,' I lie.

'You would tell me? I know what you're like for stuffing things in places. If I've missed something on the life insurance… I'm sure I made a list but I can't find that either,' she admits.

'I might have accidentally put a few letters in the bin,' I confess.

Her eyes, mouth and the lines under her eyes all narrow, homing in on me. Her cheeks dip, the bones caving in under the pressure, and I can't stop staring at them.

'But I told you not to! Why can't you just listen?'

'I'm sorry, I thought it was just junk mail,' I lie again without meeting her eyes.

'Oh, come on. You're not stupid; you know the difference. Have you been opening your dad's mail? Or my letters from the bank? There's private things in there, *private* details!' She's shouting at me now, pacing up and down the hall. 'There's no privacy in this house! None at all!'

'I haven't opened any of his mail, or yours either! Why would I open your post?' I ask, righteous in my innocence.

'If you hide it from me then I might miss something and then God knows what would happen…'

I don't know what she's on about. What would happen has already happened, surely there isn't anything worse to worry about?

'Just stop putting letters in the bin. I'm not a child, you don't need to hide things from me! I'm the adult here,' she adds as if I need reminding. I know who holds all the power and decision-making privileges in this house.

'I was just trying to help…' I start but she interrupts again.

'But you're not helping. Can't you see that? You're making things harder for me,' she says. 'I'm trying my best to keep things together and you're…'

Now I interrupt her. 'I don't know what you're on about.'

'No, you don't. And you're not supposed to, there's no reason why you should. Just leave it to me and stop interfering in things that are none of your business!' She says it like she's said it a hundred times already today. As if I'm a child. Just some toddler who needs disciplining. She's at the front door now. Clearly the conversation is over for her.

'I was only hiding the stuff with his name on because...' I stop myself.

'Well, don't. Okay?' She starts marching up the street to find the car.

I only hid them because I didn't want her to end up on the floor again, slumped against the wall, crying so hard that she had to stumble to the downstairs loo to be sick. I can't tell her that.

Another failure of a Friday night and a long and empty weekend stretches ahead of me. This has to stop, I decide, as I flip open my laptop. I can't keep pretending everything's fine when each week pushes me closer to the edge of summer and whatever comes after it. I can't keep avoiding Callie. Texts aren't enough. I need to see her.

She's been my best friend since our first tutor time in Year 7. We had to bring in something from home that would show everyone who we were. We both brought in a snow globe. When I went back to her house for the first time and saw all the snow globes on the shelves in her bedroom I knew I'd found her, found my ONE. I felt 'Here you are' as if I'd been waiting for her but hadn't realised it. I can remember Mum asking if I'd made any new friends and my answer was always the same. 'I've got Callie.' I really miss her. I miss the others, too, but not in the same way. She's not 'the others'. We're an *us*.

I scroll through my newsfeed. There's lots of photos from the audition weekend and links to more photos and stories on Instagram. Their pages are full of comments about RADA and Dublin and jokes about being the next members of the RSC or the NT. There's funny photoshopped pictures on Callie's timeline about her picking up a Bafta. Niall's standing outside the Old Vic: his parents have taken him for the weekend to treat him and I skim through over twenty sickening pictures of the backstage tour he's on. Aisha's page is full of congratulatory messages – she must have got into LIPA. I really want to write something positive on her wall, 'Well done' or 'Congrats!' But I can't make myself. I can't even click the like button. My finger hovers over the angry face. I'm angry with all of them, and it feels right. I *should* be angry.

Aisha's tagged me in on lots of photos from Dublin. I rub at the tension building in my temples, something surging underneath my skin. I know I shouldn't look but I can't stop myself. Most of them are rubbish, out of focus or too close up. I can see Callie, Aisha and me standing outside with hope all over our faces – utterly pathetic. Callie and I are together in another photo, holding hands in excitement, as Mr Davis talks in the background – totally embarrassing. Niall must have been behind the camera.

I study my face, clicking on the photo to make it bigger. I look like a phoney. I've got my fake smile on but I can see the truth in the corner of my eyes. I was nervous. I skip to the next photo: Niall and Aisha have their arms wrapped around one another in the bar on the ferry, Niall commiserating over her rejection by Dublin, Aisha taking full advantage of the situation. There's a lot of photos of them later down The Boathouse with other friends sat on benches framed by outdoor heaters and fake palm trees that skirt the edges of the beer garden. Aisha's sat on Niall's lap and she looks like she's won something. So many close-ups of them smiling, kissing one another, hugging and laughing. They look happy and so they should. *They* deserve it. There's nothing wrong with them, textbook teenagers with their perfect smiles shining out from every carefully filtered selfie.

Callie's posted on my page about the next gathering for this weekend and my head pulses. Too many 'How did you get on?' posts with smiley winking faces after them from friends who hadn't heard but would have by now. I switch to Messenger. There's loads of new posts in my inbox. As I read through them the pulsing in my head changes to fierce pounding.

Sarah-Dawn Nicholls *Soz babes, just heard the news* ☹ *don't worry there'll be others ;)*

Davina Jones *Aisha's just messaged me, cannot believe it. Bunch of idiots to say no to you.*

Emma Delbridge *You must be gutted. Chin up, chick. Something better will come along.*

Kate Bartlett *There's loads of other drama schools out there. Try again.*

Cassie Marsden *Sorry you didn't get in. I still remember you in* Grease, *you were fab;) You'll get another place somewhere else.*

Laura Horwood *Just heard from Callie. Come out anyway, it'll def make you feel better H!*

Caroline Bates *Bad luck. Keep the faith, don't give up. You'll get there.*

Aisha Begum *Hope Baldi! Get yo butt down The Boathouse now.*

Claire- Lou MacAllister *You know you are too good for them anyway. Somewhere else'll snap you up.*

And another one from Callie

Callie Morgan Otis *Please come? Not the same without you Hope, I miss you :…(*

C <3 <3 <3

And it
Is all
Too much.
Their kindness undoes me.

I delete all my messages. Posts about the audition, my nerves, how excited I am and the countdowns to how many days left before the big day are gone in seconds. Facebook asks me, 'Do you really want to delete this post?' Yes! I want to delete the whole fucking thing.

I
want
to
just
disappear.

Twitter, Instagram and Snapchat are easier to get rid of. I can see the yellow envelope symbol and the number 3 next to it but I don't click on it. I want all of it gone and with a few clicks of the keyboard it is. I am officially deactivated.

I feel
lighter,
lesser,
empty
no more holding heavy.

I google myself one last time. There are 4,060,000 results but only a few actually apply to me, mostly links to youth theatre productions, my face on the front of the Limelight Stage School prospectus and a few touring professional companies who list my name along with so many others. Just a musical footnote, a brief mention, nothing concrete or set in stone.

No
true traces

of
me.

I need to take something for my PMS pains. I reach to the back of my bottom drawer where I keep my song books and my tablets and scrape my arm on the broken wooden runner – Mum's been promising to fix it but she never gets round to it even though I keep asking. I push and pull to dislodge it, but it won't budge.

'For fuck's sake!' I start to cry. I ram the drawer into the runners.

'*Why* won't it work? Why does nothing ever work in this stupid shitty little house?' I scream. At first I feel the roar inside me rather than hear it. My blood pulses hot and hard as I start to shake, making a sound like an aeroplane about to crash land. The drawer shatters, splinters fly up into the air and shards of wood fall at scattered angles.

When my skin tears open, it happens as if it is distanced from me, in the background. Despite the ripping flesh, I keep on pushing the damaged drawer into a place it will never fit again.

The front door opens. Mum thuds up the stairs, past my room, walking into hers, calling out, 'Forgot my mobile. Knew I'd forget something! Hope?' she says with laughter in her voice, pushing my door open.

My blood drips onto the beige carpet. I don't move. My arm feels numb, buzzy but dead at the same time, like pins and needles. There's something sticking out of it. I'm panting, out of breath.

'I probably won't need it but… Oh *bloody hell*!' She gasps and drops to the floor. There's a thin splinter of wood coming out of my wrist.

'Hope! What happened?' She doesn't wait for a reply. 'What have you done? I'm taking you to A&E.' She sounds panicked. Mum doesn't do panicked. I lean on her as she pulls me to my feet. We stagger down the stairs, knocking some of the photos of all the family off the wall. One of the frames smashes but I don't look back to see which one.

10

'Self-harming. That's what it's called, isn't it?' she asks in a stage whisper, as if she's not sure if it is acceptable to say the word out loud in here. As if the scary-word police will come running and arrest her. Mum looks around the waiting room. Her hair is falling out of her hairband, bits of it hang around her face. She looks a mess.

'Mum. I'm not self-harming. I promise you.'

She glances down at my bleeding arm. She's wrapped it in a tea towel and the blood has seeped through, turning the green and white squares a strange shade of mahogany. It looks like the stuff Dad used to paint the fences with.

'Is it…? Is this about Dad, Hope?'

I don't say anything because I don't want his name in this. I don't want to blame him for something he has – *had* no control over.

'It might shock you to hear this but not everything is to do with him.'

'Don't snap at me! I don't know what's going on with you. Unless you let me in I don't know how to help.' She sounds more desperate than angry now.

I don't want to make life any harder for her but I can't talk to her about this. I know she's had the worst year of her life but I can't think about her, because all I want to do is think about me. And this makes me hate myself all the more. I don't want to put her feelings first. I don't want to think about how hard it is for her to have lost her husband so young, because he was *my* dad. He was my *dad*. But I can't say this to anyone, not even Callie. I am an evil and twisted person.

Mum looks lost. I try and think of something to explain everything but I realise she isn't going to let this go. The evidence is there on my arm and it's too much, you can't sweep blood under the carpet. Something has broken.

'It was just an accident, honestly. I shoved the drawer in too hard and caught my arm. Look, it's just a bad cut, that's all.' I take the tea towel off my arm and show her. My arm is a mess but it is just a cut, there are no neat lines, just a few manky bits of splintered wood and black-looking blood. I can see her taking this in; it really does look like an accident. It doesn't look like I've cut myself on purpose. I don't want her worrying about that as well as everything else.

'But that's not everything, is it? You're not telling me something.' Her whispered questions sound weary.

'Are you kidding me? I failed my audition! You made me promise not to try again, not to apply anywhere else, and you wonder what's wrong with me? Nothing's right with me!' I roar at her. 'How can you not see that? I mean, are you blind or just stupid? Look at me! Just fucking look at me!'

I'm standing up, my arms are flying about and she's shrinking away from me in her chair.

'This is all your fault! How could you make me give it up? And now I don't know what I'm going to do.'

My chair falls behind me. People are staring and someone in uniform is making their way towards us. There's mud on the floor: a pot plant has smashed, splattering the tiles with soil and water.

The rage is kicking in so hard that I can't see the filled chairs in the waiting room or hear the silence that has sunk every other conversation. I can only hear my voice getting louder and higher. 'And you sit there in the house, night after night, watching stupid Jane Austen films about falling in love and you go on and on about your pointless work, but you don't ASK me anything! We don't talk about anything *real* because you can't cope with the real world. You've left me in the middle of it without a map, without a clue where to go next or what to do with my life!' I shout in her face as it crumples. 'You want to help? Then tell me what to do! I'm a total failure and you take it all away from me. You keep taking it all away until there's nothing left, there's just you and me. *I hate you,*' I whisper the last bit, then I have to concentrate on swallowing to stop myself from being sick.

I can't see through my tears but I know she's no longer here with me and I don't blame her, not one bit.

'I'm so, so, sorry for shouting,' I tell her again, as the nurse pulls the curtain around the cubicle. She doesn't say anything, she just sits there twiddling a hairband on her wrist. 'Mum, I'm sorry. I mean, I'm *really* sorry.' I put as much meaning as I can into my voice. 'I didn't mean what I said.' What did I say?

'Hope, I'm trying to get it right. I'm trying so hard to be there for you. It's not easy on my own,' she whispers.

I can't remember what I said. I didn't say anything that wasn't true, *I don't think*. I wish I could remember exactly what I said so I'd know what to apologise for. I switch tactics and try to explain it to her again.

'I was trying to get some painkillers and I think the box fell down the back of the drawer and got stuck. Sounds stupid now, but things just got on top of me. I just lost my temper, that's all.' I say what I imagine a normal person would say. I can't remember pulling the drawer out or how I got so many splinters in my arm. I only really remember walking down the stairs, leaning heavily on Mum and pictures falling, maybe even smashing.

'But why didn't you tell me how you felt? If you'd just let me in, Hope...' She runs out of things to say.

'I don't know,' I reply, which is the truth.

'I noticed your light on again a lot this week. I miss your dad too,' she says the word as if they might detonate in the room. We're drifting too close to the danger zone, to an area neither of us know how to navigate. It isn't about Dad. I *know* that's not what's wrong here.

My arm has been cleaned up and bandaged by a nurse with no sympathy for me or the scene I caused. I flex my arm, wondering if it should feel quite so tight. She moves her chair closer to the bed and carefully reaches out her hand to my good one. 'We can work this out together, can't we?' As if all this mess needs is a plan or a nice list. 'Let's wait until you get your exam results then you can start making some real plans.'

'Okay,' I reply, adding, 'I love you.' How am I ever going to make this right? I'm looking at her now and can see the damage I've caused.

'Hope, you might not realise this, but I am your biggest fan. Nothing you can say or do will ever change that,' she tells me, but I wonder if it's true. Surely there has to be a line, a moment when I'll go too far and she'll have had enough? 'You've got no idea just how much I love you.' She wraps her arms around me, pulling back to check if this is alright, if she's safe to touch me now. I rest my head on her shoulder which feels like the safest place to be.

I've been here three weeks now and I have never seen him or her – the kid in the isolation room. Owen and Pryia go in and out, doctors and nurses, but I don't see family or friends going in there. None of the other kids go in there, but there's plenty of gossip which I can't help but tune into as I pack up Nikhil's instrument trolley.

'I think it's a two-headed monster and they just don't want us to see cos we'd have nightmares,' Marley stage-whispers, hoping I'll join in. I pretend I'm far too busy tidying up.

'*Shut up*! It *so* isn't a monster, you donut. It might be a… oh I dunno. Don't know, don't care. Wanna play Speed?' the boy next to her asks. Speed is this ward's current card game obsession and they're way too good at it.

I move away from them and find myself at the edge of Fatima's bed. She's asleep. She's wearing an animal print hijab today, leopard or maybe cheetah spots. The gold sparkly bits in the edging catch the light. I sit down next to her bed and reach across to pick up her book. She's only got a quarter left. I hadn't realised we were getting through *Spotlight on Sunny* so quickly, unless someone else is reading to her. For a tiny second I feel jealous. I open the book, reminding myself what Sunny was up to. I look across at her and jump, making some kind of squashed noise. She's wide awake and staring at me.

'Sorry. I didn't mean to wake you up. Hi.'

She doesn't blink. I look around but there aren't any nurses or doctors headed this way.

'Will you read to me? Don't tell the others but I prefer your reading to their singing,' she tells me, smiling.

'Thanks, I think,' I laugh.

'Not that I care, but why don't you sing?' she asks bluntly. 'Aren't you a Singing Medicine person?' She points at my top.

'Oh, um… this is just a summer job,' I tell her, opening the book purposefully.

'Yeah, but how come you don't have to sing? The job is *singing,* isn't it?'

'I'm not really part of the team, I'm only a trainee, just for the summer.'

'Right… and they're paying you for what then? To be the only member of a singing team who doesn't have to sing a note? Easiest summer job ever?'

'Good point. Reading to you?'

'You're with the wrong team then, it's Readathon you want.'

I'm fully aware I should be with the team wearing the orange t-shirt but I'm stuck with this singing team of smilers. But I'm not singing. I *can't* sing.

'If this is just a summer job where are you going when the holidays are over?' Fatima asks the million-dollar question.

'I don't know. College, maybe?' I answer.

'I'm going to college too! And then university. Mariam, that's my sister, she's an engineer. I want to be an engineer too, so I'm doing my Maths GCSE early. I want to design a better organ-donation system. Mariam bought me a new notebook, it's got squares and grids. I'm making notes and drawing diagrams so I can analyse all my ideas and theories,' she tells me, pointing at a book on her bedside table.

'That's impressive.'

She makes it sound so simple and straightforward. But what if it goes wrong? What if she fails her Maths or her diagrams don't work? Bet she hasn't thought of that and I don't want her to, because reality bites. No one wants their dreams crushed with questions they can't answer.

'What job are you going to do after college?' She returns to the question I thought I'd got away with.

'Oh, something. I've got ages to sort all that out.' I wave my hand around in the air. But what *am* I going to do? It feels hot on the ward, stuffy, and I am worn out because I can't think of a decent answer. There's nothing out there that I want to do other than acting. I've only got a few weeks to come up with a better plan – a plan B.

'What did you do to your arm?' she asks, changing the subject again.

'Caught it on something. It's just a scratch,' I reassure her with a big smile. 'Nothing to worry about,' I add, feeling an odd sense of relief as another period pain flexes its muscles in the pit of my stomach. I almost don't mind getting my period, because then I remember why I've been acting… the way I've been acting, and I feel less out of control.

'I said that's a big bandage for just a scratch.' She points at my arm. When I don't respond she launches into yet another new conversation. 'Did they tell you they got a kidney transported from another centre last night? But I didn't match the tissue, so I'm back to waiting.'

I put the book down and turn to look at her properly. Her whole body, face, arms, eyes, mouth and all the bits I can see, everything that isn't tucked away under hijab and hospital sheets, changes. 'Someone might die soon, someone who is a perfect match for me,' she says brutally.

I hide my shock. I can't imagine waiting for someone to die.

'What? You think I'm disgusting, yeah? I know it, I just don't normally say it out loud,' she admits.

'I don't think you're disgusting. Actually, I think you're really brave,' I tell her. 'I'm the opposite of brave… When my dad died, Mum told me that he was on the register to be a donor. We hadn't ever talked about it so it came as a shock. Nonno – my Italian grandad – he didn't know either and there was a lot of arguing. Mum wanted to donate Dad's organs, but Nonno wanted to bury him, to have a proper funeral and not give his son away,' I explain, the words leaking out of me. She doesn't say anything so I keep talking and talking and talking. 'So that's what I think about when someone says organ donor, the bits that are missing from my dad. I wasn't thinking about you. I was thinking about my dad.' I stop, finally.

'Sorry about your dad, but that doesn't give you an excuse,' she says. Before I can argue, she carries on. 'In France – where my cousins live – everyone's on the register. It's like an automatic thing. They've got it the right way round over there. You have to sign up to a refusal register if you don't want to be a donor.' She looks proud but angry too, like she almost wants an argument about this. 'So, are you signed up then?' she asks.

'No.' I don't bother to defend myself because what could I say that would make this alright?

'All my family are. After I collapsed in school, Mariam came in and did an assembly on it and most of my friends are now on the register and the teachers, loads of them,' she tells me proudly.

'That's amazing.'

'It is amazing! *Some* people, like your dad, are amazing!' She's getting a bit loud. 'So, are you going to go on the register now, like he did?'

'I don't know. I keep thinking about it…' I stick to the truth. I don't want to lie to her just to end this conversation. 'But I'm worried that my heart… that there'll be a problem with me,' I admit.

'Well, don't think for too long, time isn't exactly on our side,' she says. 'It isn't up to you to decide whether they're any good or not.' She opens the book and passes it to me, signalling the end of the conversation.

When I come back from the toilet, I realise I've completely forgotten to check my phone all morning. *All morning.* I normally click on the envelope, just in case a text has come in that I've missed, but this morning *nothing*. And it feels good. I press out two painkillers from the foil packet and swig them down with a sip from my Coke can. Pryia gives me an understanding look before launching into a play-by-play account of the latest argument with her girlfriend over who puts the bins out on a Thursday morning versus who does their weekly food shop. I'd go for the bins any day. I try suggesting using an online delivery service for their shopping but am met with an overly long sigh. 'If only it were that simple.' On my right Owen and Nikhil are deciding how they'd spend their lottery winnings, if they actually played. I tune both conversations out.

It's time.

I swipe it open.

I can do this, I can cope with this now.

I am reinstalling WhatsApp. It takes seconds.

So easy.

My finger hovers over the Facebook icon and the Instagram app but I'm not ready for those yet.

Small steps to start.

I check my texts.

Hopeful.

And there he is.

Excitement.

Ready and waiting.

Smile.

A little yellow envelope with a red 1 above it. Flashing and flirting with me.

Butterflies emerge from my stomach cocoon.

I open it, of course, because no matter how much I fill up my day with this place, there's still room for all my thoughts and feelings. These strange little texts are something to cling on to, as I sit in the steamy staffroom alone.

So, what's the craic? Stopped your whining and moaning yet Myrtle?

Shine on you crazy diamond,

R ;))))

SOME people might take offence at the word crazy, just so you know.

Ah, come on now, I didn't mean to sound like a gobshite. I was just messing with you.

63

Yours til Niagara falls, R 😞

Care to explain Niagara Falls? And what's a gobshite?

A gobshite is difficult to explain, it'd be easier face to face. Hands down the best word I know. Niagara Falls is where I'm headed next. You should come too and we could see the world together and I could point out all the gobshites.

Yeah, right.

C'mon, take a risk, I like to live life by the seat of my pants. I'm definitely the pilot of my plane. Hop on board?

It's a big enough risk texting you, I'm definitely not going anywhere near your pants. And you can forget hopping on board, you lunatic.

Oi! I thought we're being PC and not calling each other names. And my pants are the height of fashion I'll have you know. If you'd agree to Skyping I could show you ;)

As I text back I feel my smile grow. I look up to see Mum crossing the room. I clutch the phone tighter to my chest – a dead giveaway. I don't want her to ask because the answer isn't one she'll like.

We had the Safe Social Media Talk when I first went on Instagram. I'd already suffered the other talk. This couldn't be worse than hearing my parents explain about vaginas and penises and intercourse.

'Don't talk to any strangers. Don't agree to meet anyone. Don't go into any chatting rooms with anyone and you must not accept a friendship request from anyone you

64

don't know,' she told me, using her pointy finger. Her loose curls shook as she emphasised each point.

'And no phones at the table. We'll all leave them on the key table in the hallway, *si*? Don't want your phone pinging throughout our meal, *cara*?' Dad was more concerned about the sacred family mealtimes than internet safety.

'Sure,' I agreed, keeping my answers as short as possible to speed things up, but no, Mum had more rules and conditions.

'And don't worry about how many likes your photos get; it isn't a personality competition.'

'Or a popularity competition, *amore*,' Dad corrected.

'You know all about grooming, right? And paedophiles?'

'*Yes*, yes, Mum! Oh, my *God*!' I cringed.

'Alright then.' Mum nodded. I nodded. We all nodded. I got up, kissed them both, before running up the stairs as fast as I could, composing my first caption for my first picture in my head. The important thing was to sound interesting, blasé and super casual without being boring. I had to get as many likes as possible. I had some serious catching-up to do.

And now I'm texting a strange boy about his pants. He could be anyone from anywhere. Except he isn't really a stranger because we've met. But this is *all* I know and if Mum knew she'd freak right out. Truth is I don't know if he is safe. I don't know what he wants from me. But I'm kind of in it now and I like it – whatever *it* is, I like how *it* feels.

'I'm texting Callie,' I tell her and she sighs quietly with relief.

I will text Callie later, which will make it a truth.

'Want my advice?'

'Yes, please,' I say, in what I hope is an encouraging manner. The last thing I want is anyone's advice.

'I think you should invite her round tomorrow night. You've been very distant since Dublin. I miss her about the house.' I nod, relieved. 'Be good for the two of you to have some time together without rent-a-crowd.' I smile. 'You could invite her now, while you're thinking about it?' she suggests, pointing at my phone, so I do.

My phone beeps and she looks delighted, as if the whole world has been righted. 'That was fast!'

I know the text won't be from Callie, I know it'll be from Riley, so I turn my phone off and shove it in my bag. Mum smiles. She thinks that I'm dealing with things, that I'm listening to her and taking action. And right now, *I am*. I am dealing with things, I'm not lying about that. But the rest of the time I'm just surviving and that's a different thing entirely.

Callie stands on the doorstep and for a moment I think she's not going to come in, that she's just going to stand there glaring at me. It's a pretty venomous glare, to be fair.

'Hello stranger,' she says, lingering over the *strange* part. Her purple doc-marten boots hover on the threshold, rocking back and forth, back and forth.

'Hi,' I reply and, as she suddenly pushes past, 'Come on in then.'

'Show me the Streep!' she demands, throwing her bag on the floor. She pulls off her boots, which she's painted with signs of the zodiac in silver – they look immense. I take in her new hair. She's had it box braided again and it looks good, but she's overdone the make-up, going too heavy on the metallic eyelids, channelling Beyoncé but not in a good way.

She doesn't hug me, she goes straight into the lounge. I bet she wouldn't act like this if Mum was here, she'd be watching her manners. She's testing me, seeing how far she can go. I look at my watch as she cracks open the salt and vinegar Pringles she's brought with her without offering me one. It's going to be a long night.

'*Mamma* Erin's never out on a Saturday night, is she?' she asks, taking a break from eating Pringles. She's sat on the armchair instead of in her usual spot next to me on the sofa. That's Dad's chair and it's a really uncomfortable back-support thing.

It's Dad's chair.

'Mum's starting Pilates tonight. She's joined Nikhil's class, he's a friend from work.' I look pointedly at where she's sitting but she ignores me.

'Yeah, I know. You've told me all about him in your many texts, remember? Long texts is the new way we communicate, isn't it? Like we're just anyone.' Her words cut, as they're meant to. She doesn't give me a chance to respond. 'So, where's Meryl then?' She puts her feet up on the coffee table, breaking another house rule.

'Callie, can we talk?' I don't know what to do with this version of Callie. I've seen it in action at school and in The Bird's Nest where she works, but this Callie has never been part of my world.

'Nope, we're here to watch and learn, to see the master at work.' She fake-smiles as she picks the DVD off the coffee table. 'There's not much to say. You know it's all on Facebook and Instagram. I'm sure you must have seen.'

She slides the film into the player. 'Oh wait, unless you've unfriended me that is…'

So *that's* what this is about.

'Of course, I haven't unfriended you, don't be so melodramatic. I deleted my account, I deleted all of them.'

'What do you mean, deleted all of them? *Why* would you do that?'

'Because I'd just had enough,' I begin but she has more questions.

'Is this because of Dublin? You've been MIA since then.' Her feet fall off the coffee table as she sits forwards, closer to me. I hear something in her voice soften.

'I know, I'm sorry but I've been feeling really…'

Before I can answer, my phone beeps. I lean over to grab it.

'Oi! I thought you said you'd deleted everything?' Callie says, jumping up to grab my phone. I try and take it from her hand but she won't let go and we fight over it. She shoves me to the floor and I land awkwardly, hitting my elbow hard on the coffee table. I cry out.

She jumps on top of me. I try and push her off but she's not budging. I hear the film's trailers playing in the background.

'Get off! What are you doing? *Callie*!' I shout.

'No! I am not moving until you tell me what's going on with you. Spill or I'll read this text! And all the others too. OUT LOUD. In the street!' She drops my mobile phone on the floor and pins my hands and arms down next to my head. 'Whatever's wrong, I can handle it. I can handle anything other than you lying to me. That's what kills me. And I *know* you're lying, Hope. Don't you think I can tell?'

I want to tell her so badly. I need to tell her but I don't know how to put it into words. It doesn't even appear in sentences in my head.

'If you don't tell me what the hell is going on, if you don't talk to me then … then what's the point?'

She rolls off me. We both lie on our backs saying nothing. I sit up and so does Callie. 'I'm sorry, Cal,' I offer but it's not enough. 'I'm sorry for shutting you out.'

'It was more than that.' I can hear the hurt she's trying to hide. 'You've avoided me, you haven't answered my calls. You haven't been round our house. It's not easy to explain to Ethan why you're avoiding us. It doesn't make sense to him. It doesn't even make sense to me and I'm not autistic. Everyone's been asking where you've been and have we fallen out and I can't answer because I don't know! You're my best friend and I should know what's going on with you. *I* should know,' she finishes.

'It wasn't anything to do with you, it was me,' I tell her, aware this sounds like a break-up conversation. 'It was all about me,' I stress.

She puts her head on my shoulder, her arms around my waist and we sit there saying nothing, just holding one another.

'But you're not just a *me* – we're an *us*, remember? Promise you won't ever just disappear on me again. *Nothing's* as good if you're not here with me,' she says into my shoulder, which is now a bit damp. I guess I needed reminding of that.

'Alright, I promise.' I reach out, grab my phone and then hide it in my back pocket.

Later, after we've seen Meryl being magnificent and eaten all the Haribos, Pringles and pizza, we get my duvet from upstairs and tuck up on the sofa with Scout and finally talk.

'Hope, can I ask you something without you totally losing your shit? Are you like … *depressed*?' she asks, hesitating as she says the heavy word. And it's just a word but it's not *my* word.

'No,' I tell her, speaking the truth. 'I'm not depressed and I haven't been hiding out, not really. I've been busy working with Mum.'

She looks relieved. I wonder how long she's been wanting to ask that question.

'Then what is the matter? I'm worried about you and what the hell have you done to your arm?' she asks. 'Did you do that at work? I told you hospitals are dangerous places.' She hates me working there – she knows I can't stand the place and doesn't get why Mum's forced the issue after what happened with Dad.

'I bashed it against my stupid drawer, you know, the

broken one. I caught my arm on a bit of wood that was sticking out,' I say without hesitation. She pauses, getting ready to say more, so I stop her. 'I just thought I'd get in, you know: *Dublin*,' I whisper, telling her the truth again. She hugs me, pushing my glasses up my face at a funny angle.

'You know we were all so surprised when you didn't get through. We thought they'd got you on the wrong list or something. Mr Davis couldn't believe it. He didn't seem as surprised that I didn't get in, which was rude!' She tries to make it sound like a joke, but I can hear what's underneath it. 'So, did you get any feedback from them?'

I realise that she's been talking about me, they all have. It makes me so ashamed that I move away from her before I can stop myself.

'Oh, don't be like that, Hope. I know Dublin was different cos of your dad, but it isn't the only drama college left. There's loads of different schemes and courses and other things you can do. I didn't get in either,' she says, like it's the same thing. 'You're not the only one feeling like this, 'kay?' She's forgotten the deal I made with Mum.

'Cal, you've got your audition at the Birmingham Theatre School coming up.' I believe in her, she's an unstoppable force. 'So, just think for a second… Is there something else you want to do, for the rest of your whole life other than act?' I know the answer is a resounding NO. 'Forever. The End?' She has the grace to shake her head.

'And would you be okay with finding another way in? What if you never found it? What if you stayed as a waitress at The Bird's Nest, as a jobbing actress and never made it past being an extra on *Holby City*?' We've both been extras on *Holby City* thanks to Mr Davis and his connections, and we both want more. 'Your parents will help you, won't they. They'll make sure you get there.' I want to be happy about this, but I can't. We've been working towards the same dream since we first met and hers can still become a reality.

'You're making it sound so easy, though, like I can just show up in Birmingham and do my thing and they'll let me in. You know it doesn't work like that. If I don't get in I don't know what I'll do either. And Mum and Dad can't wave a magic wand so stop acting like I'm living in a fairy tale. I'm telling you now, living in my house at the moment is the complete opposite!' She looks upset and the last thing I want to do is upset her. I reach over and hug her.

'What's going on at home?' I ask, trying to breathe through the guilt I'm feeling.

'Just some stuff with Ethan and his TA at school. He takes up so much of Mum and Dad's time and that's fine, I get it. He's my little brother and I love him but sometimes I wish there was more space for me… Anyway, I think you're amazing. You're the most talented of all of us with *that voice*. You always have been.' She says the last bit quietly, but I hear it sneak in. Even with Callie, there's a

73

bit of jealousy there. But I don't want to talk about singing; singing is the last thing on my mind.

'I don't care about my stupid voice.' I wish everyone would shut up about my voice. Right now, I haven't even *got* a voice. 'All I want is to be an actress, like you.' I say the last bit softly because it tastes like green bile in my mouth.

'If you want it enough, you will,' she tells me and she really believes it. But I don't. We can be as *us* about this as we like but she'd choose her place over mine in a heartbeat. And I'd choose my place over hers, even though neither of us can say those ugly words to the other.

'Let's just leave it. Can we talk about something else, please?' We cuddle up.

'Oh my God, you haven't heard the latest with Aisha and Niall, have you?' she asks, knowing I haven't. Thank God for Niall and Aisha, an endless source of safe soap-opera conversation.

'On again or off again? Tell me everything!' I prompt. We turn to face each other, smiling, because this is easier. Other people's lives always are.

August

'Did you have a good weekend?' Pryia asks me on our morning break. I wonder if she really wants to know or if she's doing that small talk thing adults do.

'Actually it's been the first decent weekend I've had in ages,' I reply. She waits for more. 'My best friend and I made up. We hadn't really had a major argument but there was some stuff to work out, an atmosphere, almost worse than if we had just shouted at each other and got on with it,' I babble on, not quite sure if I'm making sense.

'I have those with Katie sometimes. I want to say how I really feel but I'll pretend I'm tired or work's a pain because the argument would make things worse.'

I nod slowly because she gets it. I'm surprised.

'So what was the non-argument about?' Pryia unwraps a cereal bar.

'Everything really, but it's my fault, not hers.' I'm not sure what to tell her.

'And now she's off to drama college?'

'Yes. Well, she's got to get through the auditions first, but she's an amazing actress,' I add trying to sound convincing. Callie deserves her place but I can't keep out of my voice the shameful notes of jealousy.

'But not you? Your mum said you changed your plans? Owen and I were wondering why you're interested in Singing Medicine. Well, I was, Owen couldn't care less to be honest.' Pryia smiles apologetically.

'What did Mum tell you?' I hate that people have been talking about me.

Mum has been filling me in on all the staff as we're travelling to and from the hospital, so I know all about the secret superhero screenplay Pryia's writing, and Owen's cello lessons not going well despite his girlfriend's help and Nikhil's Pilates classes and his growing fan base, which now includes my mum.

'Just that it didn't work out in Dublin. It'll work out somewhere, though, won't it?' she asks with the casual air of someone who's already doing what they *should* be doing.

'Not for me,' I try to keep the self-pity out of my voice but fail. 'I'm not going to drama college now.'

'But you'll think of something else,' she starts but I can't let her carry on.

'What if I don't though? What if I just drift from one thing to the next? Everything else is going to feel second best. I wanted to act, that's the only thing I wanted to do,' I admit as the panic crawls out of my mouth.

'Things change. Might take you longer to find out what your new thing will be,' she says simply. I'm so used to sympathy or commiserations, or people telling me not to give up, but she doesn't do that. There's not a drop of pity in her voice and I'm not sure how to react to it.

'Oh.'

'So, while you're working all of that out, we'll keep you busy here, but this time don't leave me hanging.' She prods my arm and I have no idea what she's on about. 'It's not easy to do a round when one of you has forgotten to sing!'

I don't have anything to say so I keep quiet.

'When you've been on the wards with us a few days more, you'll get to know all the songs we sing and then you won't have an excuse.' I wonder if she's joking but when I look at her face it's pretty clear she isn't. She's on to me, but I've got nothing for her: no words, no information, no real explanation. I just can't sing. My voice has gone and I've no idea when it'll come back, if it'll come back. I follow her back out to the ward, to a sterile stage where there's nowhere to escape, no lines or costume to hide behind and no make-up to transform me into someone else.

15

So I've been thinking, it might be fun to play a game.

Sure, let's play the Shut Up game.

You go first.

Dies laughing I meant a guessing game.

Okay.

Steady there, hold back that enthusiasm now. I'll go first, is your favourite colour black?

No, obviously. Up your game!

Pink?

Everyday sexism.

So that's a no then?

It's green, the colour of the Mediterranean Sea. I bet yours is black.

How did you know? You're like Yoda. The force is strong with this one.

You were dressed head to toe in black on the ferry. And don't go all *Star Wars* on me. I won't get half the references because I've only seen *The Force Awakens*.

You need to go back to the start, I can't believe your dad hasn't given you a proper film education. What's your man playing at?

I haven't got a dad. And again, ever heard of Everyday Sexism? Maybe my mum is a *Star Wars* fan.

Shite. Sorry. I mean, about your da.

Thanks. And fyi my mum hates *Star Wars*.

So… what are you doing at work?

Emptying bedpans.

Jayziz, sounds like you're right up Shit Street. All those germs. You can keep your piss and puke and pans.

Jokes. Lots of washing hands and cleaning gel. I smell like a doctor's surgery, not a whiff of wee.

I'm glad my phone doesn't have scratch and sniff ;)

I don't think you're supposed to insult someone you're trying to play games with.

Are we playing games here? Is that what we're doing? C'mere then so I can sniff you down the phone!

Any more talk of sniffing or scratching I'll turn my phone off.

Alright, I'll try and find me manners. God you're stubborn.

I'm not stubborn. I just don't respond well when people tell me what to do.

It's as if you've a mind of your own. Next you'll be telling me you're one of those raging lady feminists.

WE DON'T RAGE! And we're women not ladies.

Stop shouting Miss Caps Lock. I can hear you all the way from Dublin.

It's Ms Caps Lock to you, Dublin.

You do know I don't actually live in Dublin. I live on a farm. So really you should be calling me Clogherhead. Or y'know, Riley's fine.

'You're always on that thing!' Mum says, as she switches the windscreen wipers on again. The rain keeps stopping and starting – another classic British summer. 'Put the radio on, love,' she suggests. I stop texting Mr Clogherhead – whatever that means – and put my phone away. 'How do you and Callie not run out of things to talk about? You're always texting each other,' she says longingly, as if she's missing out on something. The Beatles are on the radio and she hums along, but I can tell she's building to something.

'What do you want to talk about then, Mum?' I prompt. She shrugs her shoulders and I feel like the parent. 'I heard you on the phone last night to Nonno, by the way.' I wait.

'You shouldn't be eavesdropping…' she starts, then stops and looks guilty, realising I've heard what she told him.

'I wouldn't need to eavesdrop if you ever talked to me.'

'Don't be so over the top,' she says, eyes still firmly on the road ahead.

'Why did you tell him that he can't stay with us? He could stay in the spare room if we cleared it out. We need to go through Dad's stuff anyway. It can't sit in there forever.' I've been wanting to suggest this for months. Nonno's choir tour is the perfect excuse.

I hate the spare room. It used to be Dad's music room but now I call it 'the spare room' as if it's nothing to do with him anymore. It's become a dumping ground for boxes full of him: boxes of papers, books, letters, sheet music and clothes that used to smell like him. It just smells of cardboard and silence now. I didn't know silence could smell.

'No,' she says quietly, shaking her head. Her hands are clutching the steering wheel. Her wedding ring is too loose for her these days and she twiddles it round and round with her thumb. I wonder if she'll ever take it off. 'I can't face him, yet. We've only just started talking again,' she confesses.

'But wouldn't it help if he came to stay? Wouldn't that make things better between you?' I ask.

'No. He'll remind me of your dad and I can't cope with that. Not yet. Hope, don't push me on this. Nonno and I didn't part well, some of the things I said… Maybe we could go out there next summer?' she offers, but we both know we won't. I don't think she'll ever go back to Italy, not even to visit Dad's grave. I can't believe I still haven't seen Dad's grave. It feels wrong.

'But Nonno wants to come now, he's already bought his ticket. He skyped me. He'll only be staying with us a night or two at a time. His choir are performing across the country on this tour, not just Birmingham and Cardiff. I need to see him and not on a screen,' I admit. I've missed him, it's nearly been a year.

'Oh,' she replies, looking at me quickly. 'Sorry.'

'I don't want you to be sorry, Mum. I want you to do something. Go somewhere, make a decision, come up with a plan.' I wish I could take my own advice.

'Can we talk about this over the weekend? It's been a long week and I'd just like to get through this traffic, okay?'

Before I can answer, she switches radio channels to the news. A report about how five times more money is spent on studying the causes of erectile dysfunction than on PMS gets my attention straight away – clearly penises matter more than periods. I watch Mum to see if she's listening. This might be a way into the other conversation we need to have, the one where I tell her what's actually going on with me, but she's totally tuned out. I open my mouth then close it again. This could have been a moment, *the moment,* but what chance do I stand when even a discussion about erections, or the lack of, doesn't create an awkward mother-daughter moment? She's so wrapped up in *getting on* and *getting through* that she can't see what's really going on.

'Are you listening to this?' I ask. She mumbles something about a road diversion. I give up. I guess it's easier this way because if she can't talk to me about her stuff then I don't have to talk about mine. I don't need to tell to her that my monthly calendar is divided up into some kind of Jekyll and Hyde before and after experience. That there's something really wrong with me and it's been getting worse every month. Even thinking this sentence in my head terrifies me.

No wonder I can't say it out loud.

16

'Bye!' I shout up, timing my exit with her shower.

'Wait! Hang on a sec!' I hear her get out of the shower. I stand, house keys in my hand, trying not to look too impatient. She runs down the stairs, water dripping on the peeling wooden banisters. 'Where are you going?' She wraps the towel around her chest a bit tighter.

'Into town with Callie.'

'Hope, about last night, in the car. After you went to bed, I phoned your grandfather. I told him to come.' She wraps her other towel around her head like a turban. When she stands back up, she looks different without her long hair to frame her face, more vulnerable, especially without her make-up. I drop my bag and keys on the floor and hug her tight and a squeal of excitement pops out of me. She laughs. 'So, I'll see you later. Maybe you and I could do something together tomorrow, if you're not busy with Callie?'

'Sure. We could take Scout for a river walk?' I offer, knowing this is her favourite.

'And have Sunday lunch at The Riverside?' she adds as if this is an everyday moment but it's not.

Callie lives two stops away so when I get on the bus I put my bag down on the seat next to me, saving it for her. The bus is always busy on a Saturday morning and I don't want some stranger sitting next to me, especially not some man with his legs spread wide. I wish they made more single seats on buses.

Callie waves to me as she shows her bus pass. She throws herself into the seat next to me and sighs dramatically. I'm supposed to ask her what's up but instead I just smile. I have some gossip of my own for once. She reads me like a book, forgets her news and prods me in the ribs.

'What's that smirky smile about, Hope Baldi?' She waits, eyes sparkling. I instantly wish I hadn't started this.

'You have to swear not to tell anyone else. Swear it on our snow globes?' I can't stop myself, I want to hook her in, to tell her something so big and secret that she'll look at me the way she looks at Aisha, Niall or the others when they share some juicy detail about their weekend. Callie knows every single thing about me; there's nothing left that will make her gasp. At least she *thinks* she knows everything about me.

'Our snow globes? Oh, I swear. I *swear.* Tell me!' she squeals, forgetting about the rest of the bus and the volume of her voice. She pulls me in so close that I can almost taste her Japanese cherry-blossom perfume.

'I met someone.' I'm not sure how much I'm going to tell her. She switches her phone off. 'He's called Riley, he's Irish and he's been texting me. *A lot.*'

'By the power of the snow globes!' she shouts, then looks around the bus, embarrassed for a second. 'Could he be THE ONE?' she whispers. 'When did you meet him? And where?' Her questions form a pushy queue, all demanding to be answered. 'Is he a hot patootie?'

'Um, yes. I mean, yes he's hot and shut up about THE ONE!' I cringe but cannot turn the corners of my mouth down.

'Now, how hot are we talking here? On a scale of warm to *damn hot* where are we?' She's not even joking.

'Don't objectify the poor lad!' I pretend to sound shocked.

'Good point, there's no room for double standards. Instead, tell the viewers, where did you meet and how come you've been so cloak and dagger about it?' She curls her fist up like a microphone.

'Well, Callie, thanks for asking. We met on the ferry, on the way back from an exotic trip to Dublin.' I stick as closely to the truth as possible.

'I see. And tell us, we're all dying to know, is his accent as gorgeous as Niall's?

'It is indeed.'

'*Ah*, Hope, you always get all the luck.' She drops her fake microphone. I catch her words and hold them close and wonder if that's really how she sees me.

'Well, you were inside and I was outside and we got talking and he gave me his number,' I continue casually, missing out the how and why we met on the ferry and skipping to the good bits that will keep her hanging on.

'And then once he started talking to you that was that, I'm guessing?' Callie nods in satisfaction, as if she can see the moment playing out in front of her. I don't want to ruin it.

'*Si, signorina*, as we both know I have the gift.' I wink.

'My, my, Hope Baldi, you're back!' She looks relieved and then impressed and I absolutely love this feeling. 'Ah, how I've missed you! Let me count the ways.' She hugs me dramatically as if we've been parted for months.

'*Shut up*! I haven't been anywhere.' I pretend to misunderstand. I know what she's on about; I've been missing in action for some time now. 'Anyway, he's really funny and flirty and messages me way too much.'

'So, when do I get to meet him? I'll need to make sure he's good enough for my Hope.' She closes her eyes and fake swoons back into her seat.

'We haven't talked about meeting up. Well, *he* has but *I* haven't agreed to anything,'

She senses weakness – she knows me far too well.

'Maybe you should ask him over here? Then it'll be on your terms and your turf.' She presses the bus's stop button.

'Maybe. Anyway, I know what I'm doing,' I lie. I have absolutely no idea at all. 'And it's not as if Riley's a stranger. We have met, remember?' I try to look as confident as I sound.

'Okay, but promise me you won't do anything without telling me first?' she bargains as she follows me down the aisle. 'Have you still got that app on your phone?'

I know the one she means – Stay Safe or something. Our mums made us put it on our phones when we first started going for auditions so that we'd always know where the other one was.

'Yeah, yeah, *mamma mia!*' I joke, stepping onto the busy pavement, dodging people and pushchairs. There's no danger of Riley and me ever meeting up. It isn't *that kind of thing*. I've just made it sound like *that kind of thing* to Callie. I've got no idea what THE ONE even means, let alone what he or she might look like. All I know for sure is that Riley couldn't be further from THE ONE if he tried. So why did I let Callie think he might be?

'Callie and the others are going to the theatre tonight,' I mention as we pull out of the supermarket carpark after our weekly Wednesday shop. 'I might go with them,' I add in my 'I can take it or leave it' voice.

'Lovely! What are you going to see?' Mum asks.

'Dunno. Can't remember.' Of course I can remember. I've been desperate to see Frantic Assembly's production of *The Curious Incident of the Dog in the Night-Time*. Since Dublin, the theatre's the last place I want to go but I'm not turning down another olive branch from Callie.

'I'm out tonight too,' she tells me, before indicating to turn into our road.

'But you don't go out on Wednesdays.' I fail to keep the surprise out of my voice. 'Today's Wednesday,' I add, in case she didn't know. 'It isn't book-club night.'

'Hope, you've a memory like a sieve. I'm starting my evening class tonight. I did tell you last week.' She reverses into a space as close to our house as she can get. I wait for her to switch the ignition off.

'Err, no, you didn't actually, Mum,' I reply, searching my memory banks. I'd have remembered this because this is new and Mum doesn't do new.

'Well, I did,' she says, letting out a massive sigh. 'Do you know, sometimes you look at me as if you don't even know who I am, let alone listen to what I've said,' she says it gently as if it's a joke. But neither of us are laughing. She opens her car door too quickly, slamming it shut before I've even taken my seat belt off. She opens the boot, dragging out the food. I reach in to help her but there's only one bag left. It's taken her a while to get used to shopping for two instead of three. The local foodbank did well out of us for a bit.

'What's the class on?'

'What?' she asks over her shoulder as she unlocks the front door.

'What evening class are you taking?'

She puts the bags up on the kitchen counter and switches on the kettle. She raises a cup to ask if I want one too. I nod then shake my head and she looks surprised.

'I'm trying to cut down on caffeine. I read somewhere it stops you sleeping,' I mumble.

'Are you still having difficulty getting to sleep? Maybe we should make an appointment with the GP. If I can get past the bloody receptionist that is. Do you know you have to ask her to make an appointment for a doctor to phone you? Then when the doctor phones you they decide if you need an appointment. Then if you're lucky you have to sit in the surgery for hours on end. The whole system's ridiculous!' She's on the verge of a full-on NHS rant.

'Anyway... back to you and your exciting evening class?'

'Languages! Thought it was about time I did something for me.'

For some reason it hurts, as if all the things she does are just for me rather than us. Like *I'm* the thing that's stopping her from going to some evening class, from getting a life, from moving on.

'Which language?' I ask because she's being so shady about it.

'Italian,' she says, her head in the fridge.

'*Italian*?'

'Yes. Why the face and tone?'

'Because you never wanted to learn it before...' I want to say, 'What's the point of learning it now? Isn't it a bit late for that?'

'I'm going up to have a bath and a read – that *Dark Wood* book is getting really good. They're about to play hen-night party games and I have a feeling it is about to go horribly wrong,' she says as if some made-up story is what's important here.

'But...' I start but she talks at the same time.

'That's enough, Hope!' she snaps. She's lost her control,

it's gone for a split second and we both see it. She rescues things by launching into Mum Mode. 'Have a good time at the theatre and take your key because I'm not sure what time I'll be back.'

A good time? Has she really no idea how much it will kill me to walk into the theatre and sit on the wrong side of the stage? It's like she doesn't even know who I am.

'Do you want me to drop you off or are you getting the bus? Have you got enough money? There's some in my purse if you need more.' She never offers me more money, mostly because there isn't any. She must really want to get rid of me.

'Bus,' I start, but my phone beeps and she takes this as her opportunity to go.

'Give me a shout when you're leaving, okay?'

If this is Riley texting again he has a lousy sense of timing. But it isn't, it's Callie.

Meet outside at 7:30. Am in town with Aisha & others. See you later x

I spot Callie as soon as I step down off the bus. She's standing outside the theatre surrounded by most of our theatre studies group. This is going to be deeply weird. I haven't seen any of them since the exams and there wasn't exactly much chance to talk then. Callie sees me and waves two tickets. She envelops me in a massive hug and a cloud of cherry perfume and she feels like home. My phone buzzes.

'Is that him again? THE ONE? The Irish rover?' Callie asks with a huge grin on her face and I can feel myself mirroring her.

'What's an Irish rover? Are you getting a puppy, Hope?' Niall asks.

Callie cracks up with laughter.

So she hasn't told Aisha or Niall. She's kept her word.

'So who's this THE ONE then? Is that why you've been ignoring all my calls? There was me thinking I'd done something wrong.' Aisha nudges me. I can hear the soreness in her voice and I want to deny it. 'I told you, Niall!' she declares triumphantly. 'Wasn't anything to do with acting. It was about a boy, wasn't it, Hope?' She winks at me, like we're part of some special club.

I want to tell her no, this has nothing to do with some boy, but I can't. We're back, me and Callie are back to *US*, so I grin back sheepishly and answer them all 'Yes!'

When I get home the house is in darkness. I find a note on the kitchen table. Mum's writing looks blurry although that could be the vodka and cokes Niall bought me in The Boathouse. He's the only one who always gets served without question, especially if we go there during Aidan's shift. Aidan has a bit of a thing for Niall which Niall plays beautifully, despite the face on Aisha.

Don't wait up.

Hope you had a good time.

Mx

I don't know where she is. I call her mobile but it goes straight to voicemail. I leave a message. I check my phone but she hasn't texted me. I run to the calendar on the fridge. There's nothing there for Wednesday night. I pace the kitchen, scrolling through my contacts wondering who to call. It's really late.

I open the front door and run across the little bit of

grass that divides our house from the Llewellyns' next door and ring their doorbell. They don't answer so I ring it again and again and again until I see lights going on. I hear the key in the door and the latch.

'Hope?' It's Mr Llewellyn, tying his dressing gown round his waist. 'Is everything okay?'

'No. I mean, sorry to bother you, but is my mum in there?' I point past him into his house and hear how stupid my question sounds. He looks even more worried now.

Mrs Llewellyn pushes him to one side. 'No, Erin's not here, Hope. What's wrong? What's going on?'

'I don't know where she is!' I wail. Mrs Llewellyn pulls me into their hallway as Mr Llewellyn gets the phone. He's calling someone, I don't know who.

Mum never does stuff like this. She doesn't really go out and she always tells me where she's going. I'm finding it difficult to breathe. I want to run out of their house, when I hear a car pull up outside. Mr Llewellyn walks out. I hear voices and laughter which switches quickly to something else.

I can hear Mum's voice. Mum calls out *bye* to someone, presumably whoever has just dropped her off and then walks up to the Llewellyns. I can see her face in the glow of the street lights. She grabs my hand, thanks the Llewellyns, who look confused, and marches me back home. She drops my hand to unlock the front door. I stand there in the dark, as she takes off her heels, puts her bag on the floor and her keys in the pot.

'Get in!' she shouts, making me jump. I almost run inside. She closes the front door behind me, taking great care not to slam it. She locks it and turns to face me.

'Hope, what the hell are you playing at?' She bangs her hand against the switch, flooding the hallway with light, with a violence which hurts my head. She has a lot of make-up on – liquid eyeliner making her eyes even darker. And she smells of cinnamon, a different perfume from the one she used to wear, spicier. She's got a floaty dress on, long dangly silver earrings, bracelets and a necklace. I can't think of the last time I saw her like this, dressed up, made up, wearing going-out clothes. She looks beautiful, but tired beautiful and I want to say something nice to her, but she's frightened me.

'Where've you been? It's so late,' I accuse. 'I got home and you weren't here and then you didn't answer your phone and I started to worry.'

She walks past me into the kitchen. I watch her fill the kettle.

'I said, where have you been?'

'I told you where I was going: Italian lessons at college…' She stops fiddling with the teabags and stares at me, looking worried.

And I remember. She *did* tell me. We talked about it, before I went out. How could I have forgotten?

'Yes, obviously. I meant where have you been since then, *since* your Italian class?' I try to say it as if I've known all this time exactly where she was.

As if I've known all this time that she was safe and well and not dead behind the wheel of her car or squashed by a bus or lying on the stage in a concert hall because her heart has stopped dead in its tracks.

'We went out for drinks, after the class,' she starts so simply, it must be true. She's fine. She's absolutely fine and hasn't been in any danger at all.

She passes me a mug of tea which I don't want. I take a reluctant sip. I want to take it up to bed with me and just crawl in under the covers and hide. But I can't. I have to act normal.

'…but I wasn't expecting to come home to that! You look tired. I don't think you're even listening to what I just said,' she says and I wonder what she asked me. I draw a complete blank and decide to turn the spotlight back on her for safety.

'Why didn't you answer your phone?' I challenge.

'I doubt I could hear it in the pub, sorry!' she says, as if it's nothing to her. 'What were you ringing me for anyway? Shouldn't I be the one waiting up for you?' she jokes.

'Am I going to get to meet any of these new student friends of yours?' I change the subject.

'Ah, Hope, it isn't what you think. Is that what this is all about?' She sits down at the table next to me and blows

97

too hard on her hot tea. It bubbles up. 'I can't believe you bothered the Llewellyns with this. We'll have to say sorry in the morning. Maybe you should take them some flowers or a bottle of wine.' She looks in the wine rack to see if there's anything decent there.

'Why are you suddenly taking Italian lessons?'

'Nonno. He's insisting that we go and visit them – him and your Aunt Gianna – in Italy for Christmas. I don't know the language and I don't want to get lost with you in the hire car and end up being mugged or worse at the side of the road in the middle of nowhere. *I* have to take care of us now, so the least I can do is speak the bloody language! I have to be able to look after you properly and I can't do that if I can't speak Italian. I have to be able to protect you, *it's all up to me!*' she shouts.

I jump out of my chair and put my arms around her as her sobs rip at my insides.

'Please don't cry, Mum. We don't have to road trip it like Dad always did. We can just fly. And I've got an app on my phone that can translate everything for us, it's easy. I'll download it to your phone too, then you can get used to it. We can do all this kind of stuff together, *together.*' I hadn't realised she felt like this, so on her own.

'We need a break, don't we? Actually, I'm not too bad at Italian. I never bothered really when your dad was here. But he's not here, is he?' She takes a massive gulp of her tea to stop herself from either crying or saying any more.

I'm not sure which. Her mascara has run. She looks like the end of a long night, tired out and a bit smudged.

'So, we're definitely going to Italy. You and me, yes?' I whisper.

'Yes, it's done now. We're going,' she sounds terrified and relieved. 'Now, do you want something to eat?' she asks, moving neatly back into Mum mode. 'Or is that a daft question?'

When I climb into bed later – after we've had cheese and biscuits and listened to Dad's Carol King and James Taylor album – I check my phone.

Are you awake? Whatcha doing?

Tell me funny things and entertain me. Got a hangover already and I haven't even gone to sleep yet.

What's all this talk of hangovers? Was drink taken? Was the craic mighty?

Drink taken where, outside? Talk properly. And what's mighty craic? Do you mean crack?

Dear God, do you not know how to spell woman? Why don't you use your old friend Google and find out what craic is.

Went to see a play then went to the pub. You?

Went straight to the pub. I'm locked.

Locked out?

Na, you know, like locked, drinks-wise. Don't really feel like spending another day on the farm tomorrow with me head up a cow's arse. Rather be out there, seeing the real world.

A cow's arse? You can't just chuck in a reference to a cow's arse like that. Are you pissed?

C'mon now, I've told you we live on a farm, course I have, you've just not been paying attention.

You're a disgusting chauvinistic pig!

Flatterer but I'm on a dairy farm not a pig farm. Now, have you got over yourself yet?

What do you mean?

The whole I want to be famous and go on the stage caper.

I never said I wanted to be famous. And I've already told you I went to the theatre tonight. It nearly killed me.

Cop on, woman, and stop with all the self-pity shite. Going to see a wee play isn't going to kill you. Try out for another drama place.

You don't try out, this is theatre not athletics. You audition.

Audition then. Chicken?

I never said I can't do it!

Then what's stopping you. I wouldn't let anything get in my way, that's 4 sure.

Really? When are you off on your travels then?

She shoots, she scores. Back of the net.

You started it.

Alright, truce? Now, there's arses out there that need my attention come the morning. Yours isn't too bad if I remember rightly although I could do with a wee picture, just to tide me over?

Not on your life and less chat about arses, thank you.

Text me tomorrow and I'll tell you all about the dirty cow I spent the day with.

I can't wait. I'll be sitting by my phone all day awaiting your wit and Irish charm.

Challenge accepted. Fair warning mind, you won't know whether to swoon or sext me once I unleash my charm offensive on you.

Yeah, offensive is about right. If you're sexting tomorrow I'll be blocking ;)

OH MY GOD SHE USED A SMILEY FACE! SHE HAS GONE EMOTICON CRAZY. Where will this madness lead? Next there'll be LOLing and FMLing. Maybe you're the pissed one?

Go and find your dirty cow, some of us have to be up for work in the morning.

C'mere, that's not all that's up in the morning.

Thought you said charm not smarm.

Noted. Night, Ms CAPS LOCK ;) ;) ;)

Night, Dublin.

'How come they finally let you in through the door?' Callie asks. I hesitate. We aren't supposed to talk about patients outside of hospital. Mum has drummed this into me from the start, about respect and patient confidentiality, but I really need to talk to someone. 'Hope!' Callie waves her fingers in front of my face.

'I don't know. I guess Pryia thought I could handle it?'

'She's obviously seen what you're made of,' Callie nods.

'When I got into the room there wasn't anyone in the bed.' I pause to sip my hot chocolate.

'Where was the patient?' Callie stirs the straw in her chai and banana milkshake. 'Oh my God, were they dead? Is that why the bed was empty?' She's talking like this is a book or play instead of someone's life and I don't really like it. 'I don't think I could cope with dead people...' She stops herself just in time. I don't want this conversation to be about Dad.

'No! The patient wasn't dead! You're such a drama queen.'

'You're the drama queen, spinning this story out like some scene from a play.' She rolls her eyes.

'Alright, so there was a chair with wheels and a bit of a desk or table attached to it and a boy was sat in it. I didn't know it was a boy to start with, could have been a girl, but his mum said his name.' I take care not to say his name.

'And? What was his name? How old is he?'

I shake my head, sip my drink and play for time. She isn't going to get this.

'I can't tell you his name. You don't need to know anyway. He's probably about Ethan's age, eleven?'

'You can totally tell me his name because I'm never going to meet him or his mum, am I? I swear on the snow globes.'

Our friendship is still at that fragile, brittle stage when we've made up but the walls could come tumbling down at any moment. I know she doesn't like me having this other life, being part of another world that has nothing to do with her, but I am not budging. I can't, not even for Callie.

'I need to talk to you about this, so stop going on and just listen,' I tell her.

She looks surprised. She'd been expecting me to cave.

'He was half stood, half sat on this strange chair, shaking. His body was bandaged, so there wasn't much skin on show. I guess his burns are pretty bad.' I close my eyes for a moment, picturing that first look at Kofi.

'Hope, I don't think I can hear any more. To be honest, it's making me feel a bit sick,' Callie flaps her hand to bat away the image I've conjured up. 'Maybe Aisha would be better at this kind of thing?' This is really upsetting her. I wonder if Kofi's age is too close to Ethan's and she's worrying about all the things that could happen to *her* little brother. 'Sparing me any graphic details, what happened to him?'

'They don't tell us. We're there to sing with them and distract them and make them feel better, not ask them questions about their health.'

Callie shakes her head as if this is the last straw: she thinks I'm keeping things from her.

'Poor boy. I don't know how you stand it in there. Why don't you come and work here with me? I don't know why I didn't think of it before, it'd be ace!' Callie gestures to the coffee shop and the sign on the wall. I skim read it.

Staff Wanted, Come and Join The Bird's Nest team. Must have experience in the industry. Come and get in touch, ask for Evie.

'But I don't have experience in the industry. I haven't got experience in anything apart from babysitting for the Chaudris,' I protest.

'Hope Baldi, I've been working here every weekend since I turned fourteen, don't you think I can get you in? *Course I can*! I don't like the thought of you in that hospital with all that blood and germs. And those dead bodies.' She

104

looks frightened. Her break is going to run out in a few minutes and all I've done is freak her out.

'Callie, I'm fine, there are no dead bodies. Well, there are, obviously, but I haven't seen any,' I try to reassure her.

'Uh huh, I'm going to get you another slice of cake.' She busies herself with cleaning the table, putting our cups onto a tray and lifting it with one hand, leaving behind the scary pictures I've painted, as if she could simply wipe them away like the crumbs with her cloth. A few minutes later she's back with my cake and more persuasion.

'I've just had a word with Evie and she says there's definitely room for you here, she always wants holiday staff. You're here for the live music nights anyway. Evie says you can do a solo session if you like and sing some of your own material, come on now, you can't say no to that! And you might as well get paid while you're at it. You could do my holiday cover!' She sounds delighted, completely missing the point of our conversation. This place is so her, with baked-bean cans hanging from the ceiling instead of traditional lights, the roof covered with wicker or willow with little birds hanging from it, old Marmite jars instead of sugar pots and someone nearly always playing something jazzy on the piano. 'Much better for you than being with all those ill people. I don't think it's good for someone like you,' she chatters on, as I sit in silence, listening to her rearrange my life into a slightly better version for her.

'Someone like me?' I whisper. 'What do you mean *someone like me*?'

'Oh, don't take offence, I didn't mean it in a *bad* way. It's just you take things to heart and you worry about everyone else's feelings all the time. But that's just because you're so lovely. To be honest, I think you'd be happier working somewhere else. And we'd get to be together all the time!'

She's right, I could take it easy and fill in here and just wait until she comes home from her holiday to pick up where she left off. I *could* but I'm not going to.

'Nah, I'm alright thanks. I've probably made it sound worse than it is. And Mum needs me.' I pull out the well-worn Mum card and Callie backs off, as I'd known she would, and I feel a little bit guilty.

'I bet it is as bad as you've made it sound and it'll get worse you know. But if you think you can handle it? Anyway, you're coming back tonight, right? Everyone'll be here for open mic. You'll kill it, and it'd make up for bailing on me in The Boathouse the other night. I'm not singing with Aisha again, she's such a crowd pleaser. C'mon, we can sing one of your songs, I bet you've got something new to showcase?' she challenges.

'I can't. I've got work in the morning.' I get up to leave.

'*What*? Hope Baldi turning down a live singing session? Have you caught something from that hospital?'

'I'm fine Callie, just tired,' I lie. I'm not going into

whatever the hell is going on with my voice, or lack of voice, with her right now.

'Alright, but next time, yeah?' She sounds needy, which surprises me. She hugs me before crossing the restaurant to take someone else's order. She doesn't want to hear about Kofi and I didn't even bother mentioning Fatima to her because Callie and I have already had the organ donation argument many times and we don't need to go there again. Maybe there's someone else I can talk to. I text and walk to the bus stop, making tonnes of spelling mistakes along the way.

Need tto atlakt had a weird day at work.

Riley texts back as I sit down on the bus.

The first thing we need to sort out is your shocking spelling. Jayziz! It doesn't matter what kind of a day you'd had at work, you can't go letting your standards slide like that. First your spelling slips, who knows what'll be slipping next ;)

Another text comes in before I have a chance to reply to the first one.

Look, we could get you some help you know. I could be your private tutor, 1-1s are my thing. There's so much I could teach you, young Padawan.

Normally I'm a big fan of your *Star Wars* banter but is there any chance of you taking things seriously for a second?

Chill bambino (you are Italian right? You look Italian, bella!) tell me everything.

There's this boy on the burns ward. He has bandages

right the way across his chest and he can't sit or stand or walk properly. He's in this room away from all the others on the ward. Pryia and I go in and sing with him, except I can't. I just stood there trying not to stare like a kid.

Hold it right there, back the truck up a second! Who is this Pryia one?

A girl/woman at work. Anyway, I know we'll be going back in to see this boy and I'm really nervous.

Could we talk about Pryia a bit more, y'know just so I can picture your work environment? Have you any photos of this girl/woman you can send over in the interest of full disclosure like?

I'm not supposed to talk about any of this, not even say names.

I won't tell a soul. Boy Scout's honour.

I should add in the interests of full disclosure that I was kicked out of Scouts. I can't go into it here and now for legal reasons.

Stop being a dick! I'm serious, what do I do?

Dick? For real, is that the best you can do?

Are you going to answer my question or not?

Challenge accepted. You've to think of that poor wee fella and what's happened to him and stop moaning.

Don't hold back there will you.

You picked this job, if you can't take it or don't fancy honking out a tune every day then just leave and get another one. Just walk out.

I can't.

Well shut up then, get on with it.

No, I mean I can't get on with it. I can't sing.

Why not? I don't get it. How can you be working with those singing types if you can't hold a tune? Is it that you're tone deaf or just a bit flat?

No, it's not that. I've lost my voice.

What? Sore throat like? Get some whiskey down you.

No, I mean I can talk and stuff. I just can't sing. When I try I get this strip of wood across my throat, like something's blocking it.

Okay, you're sounding a bit freaky now.

Forget it.

Maybe you need to get checked out by someone. I'm no doctor but I'm up for the job.

Stop making cheap innuendos!

No idea what an innuendo is but if it involves making something with you sign me up. Although I'm not so taken with the cheap part. I'm a class lad.

Sure, I'll meet up with you – when you've gone through puberty. Class my arse!

And so we're back to arses. It's a pattern with you. Maybe you need help.

Shut up.

A thousand apologies. Now, what were we talking about?

I can't even remember. Clearly a great conversation.

I stop texting him, there's no point. I was delusional thinking I'd be able to have a sensible conversation with him. I scroll through my contacts list hopelessly before giving up and switching my phone off.

'Where's Fatima?' I ask two ten-year-old patients playing cards. I recognise one of them, Marley, but not the other. 'She's not in her bed.'

'Gone,' he replies.

I feel sick. There's water coming into my mouth, warm and sour like gone-off milk.

'Gone where?'

'Home,' Marley sighs, turning back to his card partner.

I walk across to Fatima's bed and sit on the end of it and wait. Why would they have sent her home? To die? Or maybe because she got a transplant? But wouldn't I have heard? I need to know *now*. Eventually a nurse I recognise walks past, sees me and smiles.

'Good news, hey? Fatima got the transplant!' He doesn't stop, just shouts it across the ward before going behind a curtain. And that's it. *That's that*? She's gone, she's fixed, mended, sent home and I missed it. I thought we were friends, which seems stupid now. I guess I won't see her again. We didn't even finish our book. I remind myself to feel happy for her, that she finally got her kidney. She'll be going back to school and her life will carry on. But someone somewhere is missing a kidney. Someone somewhere has probably died.

And I can't forget that, no matter how hard I try.

When I walk into the staffroom Pryia is at her usual post, making coffee. She points to the kettle and puts her head on the side. I shake my head remembering I'm supposed to be cutting out caffeine. I feel pleased that I'm more on top of things.

'Ooh, I need this,' Pryia says, dumping her steaming mug of brown liquid down on the table. It smells vile, like Marmite or something yeasty. I crack open a bottle of water, feeling virtuous.

'You alright?' she asks, scootching closer. As usual the staffroom is buzzing with noise and people.

'Yeah, just feels weird that Fatima's gone. I won't see her again, I guess.' I take another sip of my water, trying not to breathe in the Marmite aroma of Pryia's coffee.

'Kid on Pan? Heard she got a donor at last. All happened pretty quick, late on Friday night. I think her sister took her home. You made friends then?'

I look to see if she is taking the piss, but she's smiling in a nice way.

'Sort of.' I shrug which feels dismissive.

'Used to get to me, too, when they first moved on or got transferred or, even better, got signed off. You get used to it. Try not to get too close because…' She is interrupted by Owen.

'Come on, Pryia. We'll be late! Alright, Hope? How's it going?' Owen bends over to tie his shoelace. His bag slides off his shoulder and falls open on the floor. He swears softly as he tries to pick up the contents. Pryia and I kneel down to help him. She passes him a box of tampons with a raised eyebrow.

'Something you want to tell us there, Owen?'

'They're my girlfriend's. She runs out sometimes,' he replies without a shade of embarrassment and Pryia breaks into a huge grin.

'Well, aren't you just adorable!' She passes him his mobile phone and a packet of crisps. I hand him his wallet and what looks like a diary.

'Thanks. Come on then, *ladies*, ward time.'

'Don't call us ladies, Owen. We both know you're only doing it to annoy me and the consequences of such a course of action will result in your tears,' Pryia tells him. They launch into digs and jokes at the other's expense with the ease of people who have known each other for a long time.

Kofi is in bed but sitting in a strange position: his back isn't touching the pillows. His legs are out of the bed being dressed again by two nurses. I can't not look. His calves are covered in white netting through which I can see welts, blood, scarring and his bright red raw flesh. I am the only person looking, everyone else is acting as if this is completely normal, as if they see this kind of devastation every day – maybe they do. I look up at Kofi's face. The skin on his face is mostly black but there are tiny patches like splashes by his neck which are almost white. He's watching me watching him and refuses to break eye contact. Instead of looking angry with me, he crosses his eyes and sticks out his tongue. We stare at each other for a few seconds, although it feels a lot longer, until I eventually break eye contact. He's won the first staring competition and looks ridiculously pleased with himself.

Pryia steps forwards and offers Kofi a choice of maracas or castanets. He picks both, which makes his mum laugh. She's got a lovely husky laugh. I wonder if she ever leaves the room, if she ever gets a break. Her hair is held off her face by a bandana. There are traces of her personality in her jewellery and the nose stud she wears. Her nail varnish is worn and chipped but was once bright blue and her clothes underneath her plastic apron are bold.

'What do you fancy singing today then, Kofi?' Pryia asks him and his face changes.

'Can we sing one about space?'

I notice his t-shirt. Today he's sort of dressed, although you can see the shapes of the bandages underneath his top.

It's a *Doctor Who* t-shirt and I see a sonic screwdriver on his bedside table next to a Tardis alarm clock. They weren't there yesterday or maybe I just didn't see them in my panic.

'How about we make up a song? Give us some words and we'll write it together,' Pryia offers, gesturing to me and Owen. Kofi tries to sit up but his mum raises a hand to stop him.

'Sit still, honey. Remember what the nurse said.'

He rolls his eyes. His mum looks a bit fed up. I can imagine it isn't easy to keep Kofi still. He must be feeling a lot better than yesterday. Maybe the nurses gave him some pain medication. Whatever they've done has cheered him up.

'Tardis, Oswin, Pond, Dalek, two hearts, Time Lord, Gallifrey, Cybermen and the crack,' Kofi reels off words at such a speed I can't remember half of them. *Gone.*

'Alright, we're going to need your help, Kofi, because Owen isn't sure how to say some of those words and Hope definitely doesn't know any of them!' Pryia jokes, making Kofi giggle.

He begins to explain in a very serious but patient manner the inner workings of *Doctor Who,* listing the last three actors and the pros and cons of the doctor being regenerated. I tune out after hearing why Peter Capaldi is the worst doctor. I find myself staring at Kofi's legs again, which are now completely mummified.

'*Hope!*' Pryia nudges me to repeat the chorus of the song

she and Owen have written with Kofi. I've no idea what they've just sung, let alone what comes next, not that I was going to sing in the first place. I shake a tambourine, hoping I look like I know what I'm doing.

'*Sing!*' Pryia whispers between breaths, but I shake my head. She can't make me, even *I* can't make me and I can't remember how to write songs anymore – I just can't. I can feel her tense, but she doesn't push it. I smile at Kofi, who is conducting us with his sonic screwdriver to the strangest song I've ever heard about space and time travel.

After we leave Kofi, we head to Paddington Ward. I haven't been on this ward yet and feel nervous. Before we go in, Pryia hesitates. She's pulling an 'I'm going to have to say something' face. She waves Owen on through and leads me to some chairs perched in an alcove.

'Why didn't you sing? I know it wasn't your average song but we did write it with him.'

'Sorry,' I offer, hoping it'll be enough. It isn't.

'You haven't done anything wrong. I just wondered what the problem was,' she carries on. 'You haven't sung once that I've heard.'

'I just don't want to sing.'

'Ha! Well, that might be a bit of a problem, you know, shadowing for Singing Medicine. The clue is in the title. Is it that you don't want to sing in here or at all?'

We pause as a nurse swipes her pass and the door buzzes open.

'At all,' I reply.

'Is it that you don't want to sing or is it that you can't?'

'Can't.'

'I've read quite a lot about musical therapy as part of my degree and sometimes people lose their voice following a trauma, or...' She stops when she sees my face.

'It's got nothing to do with that.' I refuse to say his name. She thinks this is something to do with my dad, but I won't use him as an excuse.

'Your muscles will lose strength if they are underused for long enough...' She leaves that hanging there. Does she think she's actually helping?

'That sounds like a threat!' I challenge.

'No, not at all. It's just there's normally a trigger for these things.'

I wonder if she thinks she's like some therapist and that I'm going to open up to her suddenly because she read a chapter on voice therapy or trauma or whatever. 'Can you remember the last time you sang?' she asks and I know she'll just keep asking questions until I give her an answer.

'Oh, you want to know about the last time I sang? Alright then. It was in Dublin, at my last audition.'

I'm instantly back there. I can smell the sweat, the nerves and the tension and I remember. As I start talking all the empty spaces I've had in my memory are filled in, in technicolor detail.

'Hope, is it? Yes, ah, here you are, Hope Baldi. Right, can you tell us why you've chosen... erm... James Taylor?' the woman on the judging panel asked, looking down at her sheets of paper. 'An unusual choice.'

I didn't know we'd have to talk about our song choice. I was going to keep that to myself and just sing. 'I ... um, sorry...' I stuttered.

'Just tell us why you chose it,' one of the men on the judging panel interrupted me sharply.

'Right, well... It's my dad's favourite. I mean *was* my dad's favourite.' I heard bitterness creeping into my voice.

'Oh, I see. I'm so sorry.' The woman did a head-tilt sympathy combo which made me dig my fingernails into the palm of my hand. I didn't want to explain the playlist of my heart to her.

'I'm ready,' I croaked. My vocal chords were clogged with grief. The music started up. The opening chords to James Taylor's 'Fire and Rain' transported me back to our kitchen, to the music playing on the radio, the extractor fan blowing away the smell of garlic and my dad in the middle of all his herbs and spices, singing to me. I heard the guitar and the place where I should sing the first line. Instead a noise came out of my throat that was all the things I'd kept hidden, all the feelings I'd been pushing back down. The pianist stopped playing.

'Are you going to be able to sing for us? If not…' The sharp man pointed at the exit with his pen. I nodded and swallowed, but something solid was wedged in my throat. *Not now, not now.* I wiped my nose on the back of my hand and shook my head a little. I couldn't do this now. I couldn't break down here in front of these other students eager to take my place. The music started up again but when I opened my mouth I couldn't get any sound out.

'You're clearly not ready. Come back next year,' the man dismissed me, putting my sheet of paper in another pile. 'Next!' he shouted.

'*No*! I mean, I can do it. Give me one more chance?'

My pleas were met with an awkward silence and embarrassment. The woman shook her head and looked away from me. 'But you don't understand! This audition is my last chance! *Please*, can't I just have one more go? You've got to give me another go!' I couldn't convince them that I was worth another chance because I was crying too hard. No one would make eye contact with me.

I don't know for how long I locked myself in the toilet but eventually Mr Davis found me. 'Hope, you need to come back into the studio now, they're going to call names out.' He paused, waiting for me to answer. 'At least you did well with your Shakespeare monologue. I'm sure they'll take that into account.' I could hear in his voice he knew the answer. Someone might have told him about the utter state his student got herself in, begging like some kind of

120

desperado. I'd been fine singing it at home, on the bus, everywhere and anywhere, because no one asked me why.

*

Pryia reaches out to me but I move away. If she touches me I'll cry and I'm not crying in a hospital ever again.

'If you'll let me help you we can do some exercises to get your voice back.' Pryia brings me back to the cold hard chair, the alcove we're hidden away in and the smell of sanitation.

'I just don't want to sing at the moment.' I give myself a little shake and stand up.

'But the longer you leave it…'

'Just stop going on at me!' I raise my voice because she's not hearing me. She's on a mission.

'Sometimes it just comes back, you know, if you let it, if you're open. I've read case studies where vocal recovery can be just as sudden as loss, like the flick of a switch. But maybe you should talk to your mum about this? Does she know you've lost your singing voice? She told me you write songs or you used to…'

'*No*! Didn't you hear me? Leave my mum out of this. I'm not one of your loser case studies!' The suggestion of talking to Mum has me panicked. I walk towards the door but I don't have a swipe card yet. Only she can open the door. I stand there like a child with my back to her and wait, willing her not to say anything for once. Eventually I hear the buzz. I stand to one side to let her go through first. Neither of us says a word as she pushes past.

On Paddington Ward are four children in cots, babies really. They all have someone by their beds except one. He cries every time a nurse comes near him. I guess that they've been injecting him or giving him some medication he doesn't like. He keeps trying to crawl into the corner of the cot to get away from a nurse he's looking at like she's the big bad wolf.

'He hates this, poor honey. I feel sorry for him but I've got to do it.' She tries to take his temperature again while he screams and cries fat tears which plop down his little face.

'Where are his parents?' I mouth to Pryia who is singing to a baby in the cot opposite. She just shrugs. Owen looks confused but he's not getting involved in whatever this is. Pryia has been off with me for days now, ever since I snapped at her about the audition, so I know I'm not going to get any help from her. I check about – no one is approaching the screaming boy. The nurse's station is empty.

I creep over to his cot, a small rattle in my hand, and shake it gently. He turns his head and looks at me. His dark eyelashes are soaked. His eyes open wider as I shake the rattle, the silver bells gleaming under the glare of the bright hospital lights. When I stop, he starts crying again. I kneel down next to his cot and poke my fingers through the gap. He recoils so I take them out.

'Hey, *hey*, I won't hurt you,' I shush him and pass a rattle through the bars. 'You want this?'

He snatches it up instantly and shakes it quietly at first, then violently. A noise comes out of him, a giggle, which surprises us both. I clap my hands, wishing I'd brought more instruments over with me. There is no way he's giving me the rattle back now. He drops it and tries to copy my clapping, his pudgy hands banging against each other out of rhythm, then he starts crying again, squirming in pain. There is a poster above his bed with his name on and some information about him. I skim read it quickly.

'Nico? Are you Nico? Hello, I'm Hope. Can you say hello?' I whisper to him. His eyes flicker in recognition when I say his name. He has a nappy on and little else, his tummy forming three small rolls over the top of it. I want to tickle him but think better of it. He starts crying again so I whisper the words to a song I heard Owen sing for an upset child a few days ago. It's a Caribbean folk song. I'm

124

not sure if it will work with Nico, maybe it will make him howl even more, but it's all I have.

'Tingalayo, Tingalayo, come little donkey come.'

I start humming it in a lower key than Owen did. I'm not sure of all the words so repeat myself a bit but it doesn't seem to matter. Nico stops crying and his mouth falls open. I shuffle closer to him, thread my fingers through the cot and whisper the next verse. As I get to the chorus he takes one of my fingers and holds it tightly. His hand is hot and sweaty but I don't move an inch even though I can feel pins and needles building in my foot. He starts to move across the cot towards me, weighing me up and watching me all the time.

'Tingalayo, Tingalayo, come little donkey come.'

I sing the next verse softly; my throat hurts from lack of use but I carry on. And I hear harmonising behind me and the gentle shake of bells. I can't break eye contact with Nico. Out of the corner of my eye, I can see the bottom of Pryia's purple Singing Medicine polo shirt. She's standing on the other side of the cot, singing softly, matching the new tempo I've set to the song. But Nico doesn't take his eyes off me. And he won't let go of my finger, not even when he lies down and falls asleep, his tummy rising and falling.

'You sang!' Pryia squeezes my arm and leads us away, out onto the main ward. 'You *sang*, Hope!'

I am worried that if I try to speak my voice might crack or break like it did last time.

'You did it. I knew you could,' Pryia says softly, touching me on my shoulder. Her hand is hot but I don't shake her off. 'And so beautifully. I had no idea your voice was like *that*! To be honest, I thought your mum was exaggerating,' she tells me. The look she gives me makes me feel for the first time that I might not be such an imposter wearing this purple Singing Medicine top.

'Come on, lunchtime. Let's celebrate with something from the vending machine!' Owen suggests. He presses a purple Singing Medicine sticker on to my top. He slings his arms around our shoulders and leads us off Paddington Ward.

My phone buzzes again, 'You going to get that?' Pryia asks.

'No.' My voice sounds hoarse. My phone vibrates for a third time and we both laugh awkwardly.

'Someone wants your attention.' she says.

I smile and shove my phone into my bag. He'll have to wait until after lunch. Pryia has taken me to Joe's to celebrate, ignoring Owen's pitiful vending machine. 'How's your throat?' she asks, pushing the hot water, honey and lemon that she ordered towards me.

'Alright…' I croak.

Pryia doesn't keep the conversation going, she just sips her cappuccino and smiles at me, which of course completely unnerves me. I can feel the babble rising, the drivel, and am saved by our lunch being placed in front of us.

'You've been here for a month now?' she asks and I nod. I feel like I'm in an interview for a job I haven't applied for. The smell of fresh lemon rises from my water, I can almost taste it in the air. 'Your mum's a maverick. You must be so proud of her rolling out Singing Medicine in other hospitals? Hard to believe she started this whole thing in Shrewsbury with just her and Nikhil. And now she's got programmes here and maybe Leicester too next year if she wins her bid for a grant. I'm hoping to get involved if she gets the funding. We'll need new team members too,' she shares as she stirs another sachet of sugar into her drink.

'Yeah, she's been talking about it for a while now but when Dad died…' I fizzle out.

She subtly moves the subject away. 'What do you think you'll do when the summer holidays finish?'

I almost wish she had said something about Dad, that would be easier. Why is everyone so concerned about my future all of a sudden?

'Dunno.'

'Sore point?'

'Er, yeah, just a bit!' It feels like she's opened one of the sachets of salt and rubbed it into my arm. I wrap my fingers around my scar and press it hard, to keep myself together. Her eyes follow my fingers.

127

'What did you do to your arm?' Is there nothing she doesn't see or notice?

'Had a fight with a drawer – the drawer won,' I say flippantly, hoping that will be the end of that.

'Do you often do that?'

'Huh? Do what?' I reply, confused. I've lost track of the conversation.

'Have fights with inanimate objects? Lose your temper and hurt yourself?' She's straightfaced and waiting, as if I could tell her almost anything and she'd just sit there sipping her coffee.

'Yeah, more and more lately.' I pause, not sure where I'm going with this but she just waits. 'I used to think it was just PMS, you know like everyone else but…' I stop.

She reaches her hand across the table and lets hers fold around mine. Right on cue my phone starts ringing. I look at the screen. Riley. I can't believe he's ringing me. We don't do that, we don't *speak* to one another. That's not how this thing works. Not now, not when I've started saying something,

finally
finally
finally

started this conversation with someone. I pick up the phone, swipe it open without looking and shout into it.

'Just fuck off!'

The tables either side of us fall silent. I'm stood up, I've knocked over my chair and something from our table has landed on the table next to us. A woman is on her feet, soup and possibly coffee dripping from her skirt. I just want to disappear.

'You stupid girl!' she shouts. 'Look at me! This stain will never come out. You've ruined it!' Her partner, who is on his feet, passing her napkins, glares at me as if I've stabbed his wife instead of splattering her with soup.

'I'm sorry.' I am. I can't look at her and her once white skirt. I want to die.

'And language like that, too! You should be ashamed of yourself! I knew we shouldn't have come in here, full of students,' she carries on to her partner at the top of her voice.

I was sorry about her skirt and I would have apologised again, but not now.

'It's just a skirt,' I tell her, 'just a skirt, you stupid, stuck-up cow! Get over yourself!'

All the conversations have stopped, even the waitresses are paused mid-order. Pryia takes me by the arm, leading me out of the coffee shop as if I'm a bomb that's about to go off and detonate the whole place with my foul mouth.

'Have you talked to anyone about all this?' Pryia says in a normal voice, not at all embarrassed. We're sat on the benches outside Joe's. She's been back in to apologise to the woman and offered to pay her dry-cleaning bill. The snotty woman refused. I guess I'll be barred from Joe's for life now. Not sure how I'll explain that to Mum. 'Have you?' she asks again. 'Have you talked to anyone?'

'About what?' I've lost track of what she was saying. She places one finger softly on my arm, right on my scar. I pull away from her. 'No.'

She takes out a box from her bag. It is a small white box with a printed name and address on it. *Pryia Arif.*

'I've got PMDD. Have you heard of it?'

I shake my head.

'That's alright, most people haven't,' she carries on. 'It stands for Premenstrual Dysphoric Disorder and I think you might have it too. I could be completely and utterly wrong – I'm not a doctor obviously – but you've got lots of the symptoms. I thought it was just because of your audition or your dad…' She waits but I don't say anything. 'But it's more than that, isn't it?' She reaches into her bag and hands me a crumpled leaflet.

'What's this?' I ask her, not opening it. I look around. She's acting as if it's okay to say words like premenstrual and disorder out loud in a public place.

'My doctor gave it to me. Read it, see what you think and then let me know if you want to talk more. This isn't going to go away and you aren't managing it by yourself and you don't have to.' She waits for me to say something. I'm holding the leaflet in my hand. I don't want to open it. I don't know what the hell PMDD is. It sounds scary. Just

130

those big letters on their own are frightening enough to know that whatever this thing is, I don't want it to be a *thing* that's wrong with me.

'We'd better head back,' she says, getting to her feet. I screw the leaflet up in my hand and, when she's not looking, drop it into the nearest bin, among the takeaway cartons and empty coffee containers.

'Any golden moments?' Mum asks. 'Golden moments' are written down and collected for grant applications. I hold my breath, wondering if Pryia will talk about Nico. I know she won't mention the leaflet or what happened in Joe's – at least I hope she won't.

'Hope had her first golden moment today. I tell you now, Nikhil, you've never heard anything like it,' Owen declares. I take my glasses off and clean them in a very detailed and thorough manner, not looking up once. 'She's a cross between Nina Simone and Tracy Chapman with a bit of Beyoncé thrown in, isn't she, Pryia?'

'I thought I heard a bit of Billie Holiday in there,' Pryia adds. 'She sang to Nico, a little boy on Paddington. She sang Tingaleyo but dropped it down a key and sang it to a different tempo, really quietly, really deep. She got Nico to stop crying and the best bit was the nurse crept in to give him his last meds of the morning and he didn't even notice.

He was holding Hope's hand, just staring at her, and then he fell asleep.'

Everyone claps and I feel my skin flush. Mum comes over to me. She wraps her arms around me and whispers in my ear so that no one else can hear, 'That's *my* girl,' and that means more to me than all the well dones in the world. As she sits back down, she's beaming at me and it's infectious, I can't stop the smile spreading across my face. I wanted to tell her what's been going on with me, that I'd lost my voice, but I didn't, I just couldn't. My voice has always been the one steady and solid thing between us. She's always been so proud of it: it's the thing she loves best about me. I couldn't lose that as well as everything else.

On the way to the airport, Mum's concentrating on driving, so I text Callie. I'm refusing to text Riley. Even though I know I should apologise, I'm still annoyed with him for interrupting me in the coffee shop. For the first time I was going to talk about it, I even started saying the P words, but he just couldn't leave me be. He's such an attention seeker.

> **Help!**
> *What's up?*
> **Told Riley to fuck off.**
> *Already? Why? What he'd do?*
> **Just been annoying and so the host of the Riley show.**

You weren't talking about yourself again were you? Did you shove your face in all his me, me, me limelight? Ah, the mens, such delicate and sensitive sunflowers.

Cal, don't go off on one. Anyway, it's all wrecked now.

That's the spirit, Hope. You go, girl. Positive Mental Attitude all the way.

He rang me. In the middle of Joe's. Can you believe it?

No, it's like he's got a phone and he knows how to use it. Utter bastard.

Shut up. I need cinema & pick n mix but can't go until Sunday cos Nonno's coming.

Nonno visit! Cannot wait to see him, I've missed him. What do you want to watch?

Don't mind, you choose.

Meryl it is then. Sunday is a go. You got me, sweets, and I'll even throw a half an hour rant on why long distance relationships don't work session into the mix. Checking out times now CX

'He flew from Fiumicino directly this time,' Mum starts talking. I nearly drop my phone.

'What?'

'I said he flew directly this time.' She doesn't need to explain this detail to me. When Nonno and Nonna flew over, they always stopped off somewhere along the way. Nonna said it was her chance of a bit of culture and sightseeing and Nonno always went along with it. When Nonna was alive…

'What time does he land?' I ask.

'19:35. We should be there in about half an hour, depending on traffic.'

19:35 sounds weird. Airport mode. It's nearly been a year since I saw Nonno. I'm nervous about seeing him, waiting in an impersonal airport lounge for our public reunion. I know Nonno will not let the environment of passports, security guards, customs, arrivals and departures curb his emotions. He will shout, he will laugh, he will cry while trying very hard not to. He will take his hat off and put it on my head and he will call out our names like he's been waiting to say them forever. And they will sound right. Then he'll kiss us twice and hold us so tight that I'll find it hard to breathe. And in some ways it'll feel normal, it'll feel like nothing's changed, except Dad won't be there. It'll be three of us instead of five – no Nonna.

And no Dad.

'It looks the same, nothing change!' Nonno declares, setting his bags down in the hall after a quick tour of the house which of course hasn't changed because it is a three-up two-down house, there isn't any room for change. Then he notices the table.

After a while Mum and I stopped sitting at the big dining table together, it was too painful. We started eating in front of the TV, searching for something to watch that would fill the empty space. I was glad when Mum sold the table and replaced it with a small one. A table for two.

'I like it! *Piccolo*, cosy!' He is trying too hard.

Mum busies herself in the kitchen prepping vegetables, determined to cook a decent meal for the Antonio Carluccio of the family.

'So, my Hope, come and sit and tell me things, *piccolina*. And you have turned into a woman since I last saw you. You remind me of your Nonna when I first met her, *bellissima!*' Nonno pats the sofa and I sit down next to him. His skin is crinkled, like a peach left out in the sun too long but still sweet, and he smells reassuringly of tea-tree oil. It's familiar and comforting. His whiskers are expertly clipped and still mostly black, but the hair on his head has thinned and lightened a little. I can see the delicate brown skin of his scalp in places. It makes him look vulnerable so I try not to notice.

'What things do you want to know?' I know there'll be something particular that he wants to talk about, he's that kind of man. I've always liked that about him.

'What did you last see at the theatre?' His eyes shine in anticipation. I inherited my love of the theatre and music from Nonno. The summer I turned ten we went on holiday to Tintagel together, the five of us. As we walked along the clifftops to the castle we came across a coachload of Italians heading down to Merlin's Cave. Nonno led them down the cliff on to the sand.

'What is he doing, stupid man! He kill himself!' Nonna declared, with her hands over her heart as if it was beating too hard.

When he got to the bottom, he gathered the Italian tourists around him in a circle, and all at the same time they burst into song, Nonno leading them. The acoustics of the cave and the cliffs were nature's amphitheatre and the sound was like nothing I'd ever heard. They sang in Italian, something from *La Traviata*, Dad said, the drinking song. People turned from the castle towards Merlin's Cave. Tourists found somewhere to sit. No one moved until the last note had been sung and then applause came from everywhere, from up in the castle, on the cliff face and from down on the sand where families were collecting shells. All the Italians raised their hands and took a quick bow and that was it. Nonno shimmied up the steps like some mountain goat, took Nonna's hand, kissed it and led her off into the castle.

Nonno packs his pipe with tobacco, content for me to return to his question when I'm ready. He moves at a different pace from Mum. I can hear her chopping, running the tap, opening and closing the oven – the heat escaping through the crack in the door that won't seal properly.

'*Top Girls* by Caryl Churchill,' I reply.

'Ah, I hear of her. Tell me, how did they tell the tale? Set? Lighting? Was there music? An orchestra?' he encourages. 'When did you see it?'

'Just before … *Dublin*. Callie and Aisha's duologue is from *Top Girls*, so Mr Davis thought it'd be useful to see it.' I find it hard to say the word 'Dublin'.

'And since Dublin? You see anything else? I hear Theatre Severn has a good schedule this year.' He says the word Dublin carefully.

'I went with Callie to see *The Curious Incident of the Dog in the Night-Time*,' I tell him, glad I have something to say.

'Ah yes, I read the book a long time ago now. Your Nonna teased me because she said it was for children. I told Renata "the greatest stories are those for children" and she clicked her tongue at me, *pfff*. Stories are stories, if there's a tale to tell and someone to listen it doesn't matter if they are an old man with grey hairs or a child with gaps where their teeth should be,' he says, involving Nonna in as many sentences as he can. I noticed Mum avoided this; if she could not mention my dad's name then she felt as if she was winning at life. I couldn't tell her but to me it felt more like losing. It was the thing we didn't talk about, the name we couldn't say without one of us ending up in tears. But Nonno says Nonna's name all the time – *Renata* – bringing her to life as if she is in the room with us now, clicking her tongue. I can't ever imagine clicking my tongue at anyone with such affection and real impatience all bundled up in one sound. It's too personal.

'Tell me more,' he invites. So I do, I tell him all about Frantic Assembly and describe the way they made Christopher walk up walls, using the grid formation and graph-paper set design. I tell him everything I saw as I sat on the outside, looking in.

Nonno delays the big question until after our meal, waiting for Mum to go to bed so he can smoke his pipe in peace. Mum has already asked him not to smoke in the house. He's opened the back door as a concession. Mum always went to bed early to read when Nonno and Nonna came to stay, unable to keep up with the rush of Italian. Once I reached a certain age – I think it was twelve – I was invited to join them while they sipped their grappa, a drink I never liked. It smells so deceptively delicious, like plums soaked in honey, but tastes like cough mixture, sour and sharp. Now Nonno and I sit together while he sips his grappa and smokes his pipe, and the elephant in the room grows and grows until I can almost hear it breathing and sense the swish of its trunk.

'And so,' Nonno invites.

'I failed.'

'*Sì*, this I know.'

'So, I need a plan B,' I carry on, almost relieved to be saying it, to be accepting it.

'No, no need,' he replies, puffing and blowing.

'What do you mean?' I sit forwards on my chair, ready to listen. I feel excited and relieved. Just by being here he's making things happen.

'I say no. You do not need Plan B. You have Plan A and so you stick to it,' he says in short bursts, sitting back in his chair.

'But, *I can't*,' I protest. 'I didn't get in.'

'*Sì, sì*, yes, but you try again, *piccolina*, you don't just stop.' He sips his grappa.

As much as I love him, he really annoys me sometimes.

He's been in the house for a few hours and already he knows everything?

'We try and try again. This is what they say, *sì*? It is in your blood.' As if all I need to get into drama college is a blood test. If only – I'd gladly pay in blood.

'But I'm not good enough. I would have got in if I was.' I try to mirror his voice, the soft tones of knowledge and certainty, but it doesn't quite happen for me.

'You are more than good enough. I have seen and heard you, I have watched you grow. There are other doors to try if you are brave enough, *sì*? I know you can do this, *piccolina*.'

He nods his head in satisfaction. And I want to believe him. But how can I? I can't tell him what happened in the audition because I'm ashamed. He thinks I'm in control but I'm not. He's watching me, trying to read my face, and I'm so tired of hiding from everyone.

'Come here, come to me.' He puts his pipe down carefully on the table and holds out his arms. I walk over to him. He pulls me down onto his lap. I sit there like a giant doll, awkward and gangly, until he kisses me on the head so tenderly. He starts singing and at first I want to run away. I'm embarrassed, but he isn't, not for a second. And I can't break out of his hold, not without hurting him. He keeps on singing. I've no idea what about because it is in Italian, I can just about follow a conversation but singing what sounds like some old folk song in Italian is way out of my league. After a few minutes of holding my neck at an awkward angle, I find it easier to rest my head on his shoulder. He relaxes his arm a little and slows down his singing until it matches the steady rhythm of his heart and to that sound – the steadiest of sounds – I fall asleep.

'We've had a request from the nurses to see Kofi. He's asked for you,' Pryia tells me as we put our bags in our lockers.

'*Me*?' He doesn't even know my name.

'Yup, he must have heard the word on Hospital Street about *that voice*!' she tells me, smiling. She waits as if I'm supposed to say something in response. People always do. I've no idea what they expect me to say. As if I can say: 'Oh yeah, my voice is out of this world, isn't it?' Mostly I say nothing, which can come across as rude.

When we get to Kofi's room we go through the motions, scrubbing up, putting our aprons and masks on. We elbow our way into the room and stop as our eyes register the same thing at the same time. Kofi isn't in his bed. His mum isn't there either. The room is empty.

'What?' Owen's voice is muffled by his mask. He checks his chart.

'Maybe he's seeing a consultant? Or he's gone to another

ward?' Pryia suggests, but there's a catch in her voice, a nerve triggered as she looks at the empty bed.

'Well, let's go and find out,' Owen says, pulling his mask off.

'Hope, you wait here. We'll be back in a minute,' Pryia tells me. I sit down on the chair and get out my cleaning gel.

I think about what an empty bed in a hospital means to me.

I've squeezed out too much gel, the alcohol or something acidic makes my eyes water.

I think about Fatima's empty bed and her successful organ donor.

I blink my eyes clear.

I look back at Kofi's empty bed.

The door opens and people come into the room.

I think about my dad's empty hospital bed.

'Hope!' I hear a voice call out. 'What's happened? Are you *crying*?' He sounds less than impressed.

'Here you go, honey.' His mum passes me a tissue. I take my glasses off but don't know where to put them. Someone takes them.

'Thank you,' I reply, drying my eyes. There's black mascara all over the tissue.

'You look like a panda!' Kofi shouts happily and I laugh. Kofi's mum hands me back my glasses.

'Cheers, well, you look like a leopard,' I retort as my eyes clear and I spy his animal print t-shirt.

'I know, goals! So, what are you crying about?' Kofi asks me.

'Kofi! Manners, honey,' his mum says.

'I got cleaning gel in my eyes,' I tell him. 'Anyway, where've you been? Owen and Pryia have gone to look for you.'

His mum gets up. 'I'll go and find them. Will you two be good?'

'Sure,' he tells her, looking happy at the prospect of being left alone with me, which is slightly unnerving. His mum waits a second or two more and I realise she's waiting for me to say something. *I'm* the one who is being left in charge, not Kofi.

'Oh, yeah, we're good. Take your time.' I try to present a relaxed and confident front.

'Thank you, honey,' she says to me. Once she's left the room Kofi lets out a big sigh.

'Got any sweets? I'm dying for a Big Mac; can you smuggle me one in?'

'So, where were you?' I ask him, ignoring his requests for sugar and burgers.

'Oh, boring meeting with Mr Rasheed about boring stuff. Have you been to the *Doctor Who* Experience? It is awesome!' he quickly changes the subject.

'No, I mean, I haven't been yet but I will do.' I remember I'm not supposed to ask the patient questions.

'I'm going to live in Cardiff when I grow up. It's where it

all happens. I'm going to be a *Doctor Who* cameraman! Have you got any Match Attax? Or *Doctor Who* cards to swap?' He looks as if he is expecting me to whip some out of my back pocket.

'Not right now, but I'll bring some in next time. Which ones do you want to swap?'

He points to a box on his bedside table, a school shoebox from a discount warehouse. I pass it to him. Inside are cards held together with hairbands tight enough to snap. He picks one set out and flicks through it, then selects ten or more cards.

'These are my swaps. Next time, bring yours and we can play Top Trumps too. Important question alert – who's your favourite Doctor?'

'David Tennant?' I pick the one doctor I know.

'Oh, *shame*. I'm Team Matt Smith, he's the fun one and the best. Top Doctor. Fact. Tennant is second, possibly tied with Ecclestone. We don't talk about the other one.' He looks disappointed with my response. I'm lucky I didn't pick the other one, whoever he is, poor guy. Kofi puts his swaps back in the shoebox. I place it on the bedside table. I search for a new topic of conversation but haven't spent much time with eleven-year-old boys, apart from Callie's brother Ethan. I could ask him more stuff about *Doctor Who* but he's clearly a hardcore fan and would catch me out in seconds.

'So, are you going to sing to me then?' Kofi asks.

146

'Uh, well… it might be better to wait until Pryia and Owen get back. They've got all the instruments and know what they're doing.'

'Don't you know what you're doing?' he asks bluntly. 'I thought you were one of the adults. *Please*?' he carries on in a small voice. 'You can write something for me, can't you?'

'How about I sing you a song by someone else? Who's your favourite?'

'Tracy Chapman. Do you know her?'

I nod, I know her, but I'm surprised he does.

'Do you really?' His eyes sparkle. I nod again. 'My mum plays her songs all the time. It sounds like being in our flat when I hear her voice. Can you sing "Revolution"?' he asks, his eyes drooping a little. 'That's her best one,' he adds, as Pryia enters the room. I clear my throat and hum the introduction and then I start singing to Kofi.

Hey, Dublin! Where are you? Sorry for swearing at you.

Is this how we're going to communicate with one another now Ms Caps Lock? Cursing and cussing like dockers? I didn't know girls knew language like that.

Well, this girl swears, so deal with it.

And you kiss your mother with that potty mouth?

Shut up about potties, you're not American. Anyway, I've got something to tell you.

Howdy partner, now we're talking. Hope it's juicy. *Hope* See what I did there?

I just sang!

WTF? Talk sense woman.

Now who's swearing! I sang to Kofi, a kid on the burns unit.

Right, and this is breaking news why?

And I sang to Nico.

Hold the front page. I'll text Sky News. This could go viral.

Whatever, I knew you wouldn't get it. It's just I haven't been able to do it in a while.

C'mere, I haven't been able to do IT in a while either. Not many people to do IT with, out here in the sticks.

Think we're talking about different ITs.

Ah, now that's a terrible shame.

You have no shame!

Yeah, yeah. Heard that one before.

Gripping as this is, let's change the subject. What are you up to?

Selling my bike. Going travelling. Going to Finneas Fog it round the world. Might take a wee while longer than 80 days though.

Didn't know you had a bike and google how to spell Phileas Fogg. And Nellie Bly managed it in 72 DAYS! Not 80 but 72! So, you know, do your best yeah?

Sass, Ms Caps Lock! There's lots you don't know about me. I'm an international man of mystery. And who's this Bly woman?

Really? International? Bet you've never even been abroad. Again, google her. We studied her in history. She was a journalist dealing with facts and real travel not fiction.

My travels aren't fictional!

So where have your so-called travels taken you then?

I've been all the way over the sea to sunny Wales. It's another country right? I definitely needed Google translate, couldn't understand a word. Remember me now, your hero on the ferry?

Tropical Wales. Now I can see why you'd refer to yourself as mysterious. And there was nothing heroic about you. Not that I needed a hero.

Way harsh, Hope.

So, where are you going to go then, when you go on your big trip?

Somewhere far away from here that's for sure. Maybe Canada.

Original.

Give me a break? I could have said New Zealand.

Or Australia. Have you actually booked any tickets then? Or, you know, actually got a passport?

Actually yeah I have. Actually.

Alright, so I repeated a word. What are you, the grammar police? So, are you scared of travelling or is it leaving your dad?

Am I shite. Course not. You're talking out of your arse now.

We're back to arses are we? And calm down, I was only joking.

Oh. Right. Awkward. Me da'll be fine once he finds someone else to milk the girls.

I haven't been to Italy for about a year and my mum is getting freaked out talking about all the things that could happen to two females travelling alone.

I could come too. International man of mystery ready and more than willing to protect travelling females.

We don't need a man to travel with us. I have an app.

An app, we've been replaced with apps? Not this feminist shite again.

It isn't shite. Go and google Gloria Steinem. Or start reading *Teen Vogue*. It isn't too late to educate yourself you know.

What is it with you and Google? Are you on commission? C'mere and tell me more about this Gloria one. Is she a ride?

You can't view women in that way, you'll get hurt.

Now, is this some kind of secret code you feminists have come up with? Like in the yard at school when you pretend to hate someone and pull their hair but really you just want to get it on?

If there's a secret code you'll never crack it because you'd need a brain for that.

Wounded!

'Hope? Did you read that leaflet I gave you?' Pryia interrupts me, speaking quietly so that only I can hear her.

'No, sorry. I lost it,' I lie, switching my phone off as Pryia reaches into her bag and pulls out another leaflet. What is it with her and leaflets?

'Here's another one.' I fold it away but she's still looking at me.

'What's this all about?'

151

'Just read it,' she says, talking over me. 'It's about PMDD.' She knows I haven't read the leaflet she gave me outside Joe's. I swear she must have spies.

'Oh, right. What, you want me to read it now? In *here*?' That'd be ridiculous, someone might see.

'Yes, *now*! You're not leaving my sight until you've read every single word,' she replies.

I sigh and unfold it and begin. She doesn't speak or move, just sits on the chair next to me and waits. I read it as quickly as I can but there are bits I can't skim or whizz over. Some words jump on the page and look as if they've been printed with caps lock on. Parts of the leaflet have **OI! HOPE BALDI – LOOK HERE** in bold with arrows pointing to words like

→ **feeling overwhelmed and out of control ?** ←

or

→**Irritable?**←

Premenstrual Dysphoric Disorder sounds really serious. I don't want to have a disorder, let alone a dysphoric one – whatever that means. I skim over the fun list of Top Ten Symptoms:

1. Mood swings
2. Intense anger and conflict with other people
3. Tension, anxiety, and irritability
4. Difficulty concentrating/forgetfulness
5. Depression and feelings of hopelessness

6. Change in appetite

7. Feeling out of control

8. Fatigue and sleep problems

9. Cramps and bloating

10. Headaches

Great. I score a perfect 10. There's another bit which asks if there's a 'history of mood or anxiety or history of premenstrual mood dysregulation in my family'. I am not going to ask Mum about that. I start to hand it back to her but she's not having it.

'Nope. Read the bit about behavioural symptoms first.' Pryia places her silver metallic nail on the leaflet.

PMDD mood symptoms only present for a specific amount of time, usually the week before menstruation.

'Does that sound familiar?'

There's not much point denying it, so I nod and then read on.

Most women suffer from PMS at some point in their lives but premenstrual dysphoric disorder (PMDD) is different. It causes emotional and physical symptoms, like PMS, but women with PMDD find their symptoms debilitating, and they often interfere with their daily lives, including work, school, social life, and relationships.

It's not as if I've ever been normal and now it's actually official. There is something properly the matter with me. A thing with a scary name. In bold.

'My doctor gave me a leaflet like this when I was first diagnosed. There weren't any books to read, so this is all I had,' Pryia tells me, as if she's discussing what she's going to have for lunch today. She's not even lowering her voice. Anyone in the staffroom could overhear her. 'I was at university, one of my friends in the house I was sharing forced me to go and see my GP. I'm glad he did, even though I hated him for a bit. I thought I was crazy or hoped that he was. And I was mortified when he brought it up. I presumed everyone felt like me but just handled it better than I did,' she carries on, as if this subject is something people can *chat* about.

'And they helped you?' I ask, desperate to know.

'My GP, then I saw a cognitive behavioural therapist. Know what that is?' she checks. I shake my head. 'CBT's like counselling but more specialist. The aim is to change the way you think about certain things. There are all these exercises you can do and once you start charting your periods you spot the signs and can be prepared. Have you got the Clue app?'

I shake my head. 'No, what's that?'

'Get it. It's brilliant, its fem tech, it charts your periods, your moods, what you eat and it lets you know when you've got a period coming up or when you're about to get PMS. Here, look.' She opens her phone and presses on a white circle with a red flower symbol on it. 'See, it asks me to put in today's data and then there's all these other options about bleeding, emotions, how much sleep you've had, how much sex you've had or not and so on.' She shoves her phone in her pocket. 'I'd be lost without it. I've tried charting my periods on a calendar and in a diary but I always forget. That's one of the problems for me – I get a bit forgetful, well, a lot forgetful actually. Drives Katie mad. Do you get that?'

I think she already knows the answer. I nod with relief.

This is really happening. I'm someone with a problem that can be sorted out with leaflets, an app and maybe some medicine. She carries on talking. 'I was misdiagnosed with depression to start with and put on the wrong kind of antidepressants for me. Took a while to find the right ones.' She smiles as if *this* is something to smile about. 'So I stopped taking them and tried to manage it through diet and exercise, but then I had a bit of a relapse and … that's a story for another day. Anyway, a different GP prescribed the right tablets and they worked quite quickly. I'm on them now, I'll probably be on them for a long time, but that's fine: whatever works,' she finishes.

I want to skip back to Pryia's *story for another day* and hear more about this relapse. I want to ask her what she did. I wonder if it's as awful or as stupid as some of the things I've done. Instead I opt for something easier.

'What happens if you stop taking them? Have they changed your personality?' I have to hold my hand over my mouth to stop more questions gushing out.

155

'I don't know what would happen if I stopped taking them. I'm not ready to find out. Not right now. I need help and … I *think* you might too.' She stops talking to see if I'm alright, if I'm handling what she's saying. I've got no idea what to do with my face. 'You have to know one thing – none of this is your fault.' She leans in close and says it again, tapping me on the arm as she says each word. 'You haven't let yourself down, you aren't weak. You're the opposite. Just think about everything you've been dealing with, all by yourself. And the best thing is that you aren't always going to feel like this,' she adds.

'Really?' I want to believe her but it sounds like a fairy tale.

'I'm not saying that the tablets can magic everything away and I'll be honest, your bad days might get worse occasionally, but one day you'll realise that you're having more good days, I promise.' I want to trust her, so much. 'But, Hope, you have to be honest, with yourself first and then with everyone else. And you *have* to talk to your mum,' she says.

I shake my head. There's no way I'm telling anyone, especially not Mum. This would be enough to push her over the edge. She's already close enough.

'What about Callie then?'

I shake my head again.

'Your mum must have noticed what's been going on with you?' Pryia presses. 'It's not like you can hide it every month, is it?'

'She thinks it's about my dad, or drama college or both. To be honest it has been easier to let her think that. How do I tell her something that sounds so weird and melodramatic? I don't want to freak her out and give her more stuff to stress about. I'm not sure I can deal with it and until I can deal with it there's no way I'm dumping this on her,' I tell Pryia.

'But you *can* deal with it, you have to. It's that simple. It's your body and you need to own it. Coming out will be easier than keeping all these secrets. Aren't you tired of all the secrets, Hope?' she asks and she's right, I am. 'You know, the more you talk about your periods, the less embarrassed you'll feel, and when you stop feeling embarrassed you can face anything. I talk about mine *all the time*, to anyone who'll listen! I make a point of it because half the world has them, yeah? Why should we be shy and quiet about it?'

She's right. Even though she's embarrassingly loud, I know she's right.

'But it can't be that simple, can it?'

'It's as simple as you make it,' she says, not willing to let me off the hook. 'There's no need to make your life harder than it already is.'

I look around the room; people are talking, making cups of tea and laughing about something, totally and utterly oblivious to what's just happened to me, what Pryia has just said. I fold the leaflet away neatly and put it into my bag so I can read it again later. Pryia stops talking and all the buzzing and interference in my head makes way for a different noise, one that sounds a bit like hope.

I hadn't expected Nonno to offer to take me to my optician's appointment but he insisted. We catch the bus together and sit in comfortable silence on the uncomfortable seats. He's brought his walking stick with him. He'd been in denial about needing it the last time I saw him. He's dressed in a crisp, white, pressed linen shirt, which on anyone else would be creased by now, soft cream trousers and highly polished brown leather shoes which match his hat. He looks like a catalogue model with his dark skin and smiling brown eyes. I can see why Nonna put up with his cheek and teasing. He's still a very handsome man – he reminds me of Dad. When we get off the bus he takes a moment or two to find his feet and then sets off at a brisk pace, as if to say, 'I've still got it, try keeping up with me, young lady.'

Dad and I always went to the opticians together, since I was five, every check-up, every new pair of glasses, was him and me. Specs and Checks he called it and afterwards he'd take me to a café for an espresso and cake and we'd sit and write songs together in one of the little notebooks he used to buy me. I wonder if Nonno will try and do the same and if I'll mind. Dad and I visited them all before deciding that The Bird's Nest was our favourite. We used to give each coffee shop or café a mark out of ten for the cake, the coffee and the toilet facilities. Last year I wouldn't even go to the opticians, I couldn't bear it. Nonno hadn't asked, he'd decided for the both of us. Not that he needs his eyes testing, he claims they're still perfect.

'Why don't you wait out here and I'll come and meet you once I'm done?' I suggest.

He nods his head once, kisses me on both my cheeks and walks over to the newsagents. This is something I'm going to have to get used to doing on my own. Soon Nonno will be back in Italy. On my own is fine. I just can't cope with someone being there for me one minute and not the next.

I check my phone as I wait for the optician to see me. Nothing. Absolutely nothing, apart from one from Callie with her holiday flight times and a link to the fancy villa she's staying in. Her mum and dad seem to think it'll be the last year she wants to go on holiday with them so they're making a big deal of it. Months ago, she asked me to come with her. Looking at the photos she's sent me of the villa I wish I'd said yes. Too late now.

*

'How did it go?' Nonno asks when I come out. He stands up from the bench and holds his arm out to me. I notice it is shaking a little and I realise that he needs to lean on me rather than the other way round.

'Fine, no real change in my eyes so these are good for now.' I reply, fiddling with my glasses. They always feel weird when I put them back on after an eye test.

'Shall we walk along the river?' Nonno takes his arm off mine to lean on his walking stick instead. 'Did I ever tell you about the time your father ran away?' I love the fact that he doesn't talk about the weather, or what we're having for tea, or anything else that holds no interest for me.

'No!' I say, surprised. I've heard most of Nonno's stories about Dad, it's one of the best things about talking to him, his endless stories reaching from Dad's past to my present.

'Well, he wasn't a little boy, he was a bit older than you, in fact. He made mistakes in his exams, he didn't want to stay at home with us, but he didn't know what else to do. Your Nonna told him *Get a job, work things out!* They rowed, you can imagine? She told him, *Fix it, Franco,* as if it was that easy. Renata's fire was not easy to put out once lit – a passionate heart for a passionate woman,' he says softly, pausing to pick up a stick and throw it in the river and to catch his breath. We watch the ducks and swans examine the stick before moving away, disappointed.

'I bet!' I love hearing stories about Nonna's famous temper, it makes me feel less lonely.

'I left them to it, but called to my good friend, Luca, in Ireland and asked if Franco could come and stay with them in Dublin, just for a little while. Luca and I have been friends all our lives, he too has a granddaughter, Lucia. She's an actress, you know, on the stage. Luca is so proud, so proud of her.'

He passes the information to me to see what I will do with it. But I don't want it right now. I want Dad's story. *I want Dad.* I'd known Dad had lived in Dublin for a year and that he'd met Mum there while she was on holiday, but I never really asked what he was doing in Ireland in the first place. I'd just presumed it was music and study. Or maybe he needed to travel, like Riley. 'Your nonna was furious with me, she accused me of sending your papa away in disgrace. Ha! She would not listen to me. And of course, we all visit him, your Aunt Gianna too. We all stayed with Luca and his wife. I showed Renata that Franco was fine, that things work out, even if we don't know *how* they will work out,' Nonno continues, walking and talking.

'And?' I ask, wanting the next instalment.

'He told us he wanted to re-sit his exams in Dublin, so your nonna, Auntie Gianna and I left him there. Then there were the auditions – lots of them – and then he met your *mamma.* The rest you know: he moved to Cardiff to be with her, they got married and then there was you, *piccolina*. But it wasn't all smooth paths and plain sails, he made mistakes and he had to fix them.' I see where he's going. 'He had to find a different path,' he adds, in case I've missed the moral of this tale.

'So you think I've messed up my exams like Dad did?' I turn to face him.

'No, I don't say that. But I do say you can fix it. You might just need to take a different path to get there, like Robert Frost says – the one less travelled – and that might make all the difference? But perhaps you don't want to hear this just now. I think maybe you don't want to listen to an old man talking about the past and poetry.' He smiles.

I've heard enough about Dad and how he fixed things.

'What's she been in?' No need to explain who I'm talking about.

'Lucia? Ah, I think she is in Stratford now, with the RSC.' He waits.

'*The* RSC?' I check, even though I know he can only mean *that* one.

'Yes, *the* Royal Shakespeare Company,' he clarifies, smiling. He rolls the 'r' of Royal making it sound even grander. Was this whole conversation about Dad really a present, with this wrapped up in the middle of it?

'Have you been to Stratford, Nonno?'

'Not in a long time, not for too long.' He sighs, and stops to get his breath back.

'We could go, you and me? I mean, if you'd like to?'

163

I wonder if it's possible just to make something happen by asking.

'Ah, a day trip you mean? *Bene!*' I didn't mean just that. I don't want a day of boating on the river Avon or a touristy trip to Shakespeare's house. Stratford means something different to me.

'What's she in?' I delay the big question I want to ask.

'You'll never guess! They are doing your *Top Girls*! A new all-female production – director, actors, set, lighting, sound, costume, all of it! And no one else has seen it yet but I hear tickets have already sold out,' he adds with a flourish.

'Could you ... do you know her well enough to ask a favour?' I force the words out. Even the word favour sounds too rude. Clumsy. But I push on all the same.

'What is it that you need, *piccolina*? What is it that you want to ask?' he prompts when I'm slow to respond.

'Could I meet her? Or could I... maybe watch them rehearse? I wouldn't get in the way or anything.' He waves this away with his hand. 'It doesn't matter if that's too much.' He must think I'm using him to get what I want.

'Of course I will ask!' he declares. 'I can only ask, *si*?' He smiles again.

'They might not and that's fine but...' I don't know how well he knows this girl and her family.

'I will do the asking and then you will do the pushing open of the door, *si*?' He says the last bit so theatrically that the ducks scatter across the river. 'And don't worry about what to tell your mother. You leave your *mamma* to me,' he adds.

'*Sì*,' I reply happily, even though there's no need to reassure him, because I hadn't even thought about Mum.

When we get home just before lunch, Mum is out. She's left a note telling us she's across the field walking Scout. Nonno quickly begins to make Sunday lunch. He puts music on – a bit of *Carmen* – singing, chopping, washing, preparing, in his element, which releases me from his company. In my room I switch my laptop on and google workshops at the RSC. I lose at least an hour before checking my email. Nothing. I wonder what I've done, what I've said that's offended Riley. I type another one, just in case he hasn't received any of the others, they might have gone in his spam box or something. I wonder if it is possible to make something happen just by asking.

I hear the backdoor slam shut and then Scout bark. I delete it. Then I type it again.

Maybe we could meet up?

And press send before I can change my mind.

I know when I call the doctor's surgery on my Monday morning break, that it's a long shot. I kind of hope the receptionist will tell me to ring back next week and I'll be able to hang up and moan about how useless they are.

'Can you tell me what's wrong?' the receptionist asks. *Seriously*? In my head I give her an answer which if I said it out loud would probably bar me from the surgery for life. But as I'm in the toilets at the hospital, I opt for the slightly politer version.

'Um … my periods,' I whisper, completely embarrassed. This one word has its usual effect, at least it stops her asking any more questions. But why am I embarrassed? I shouldn't be embarrassed, she must have heard much worse before, surely? I hate this feeling of being on show, having to talk out loud to a complete stranger. I bet she doesn't really need to know, she probably won't even tell the doctor. When she offers me an evening appointment that's been cancelled I take it. I can't leave this any longer, I've left it too long already.

After Mum and Nonno finally leave for choir, I power-walk to the doctor's surgery, head down and ready to avoid everyone. Inside I press the touch screen to confirm my appointment, so much better than having to talk to the receptionist. I sit on the green chairs, pretending to be completely fine with sitting in a room full of strangers, before going into a smaller room to tell another stranger all the vile and hideous things that are wrong with me. I take my phone out and email Riley.

I'm at the doctors.

He likes a hook, something to grab his attention. Hopefully this should do it. I'm so bored. I look up at the screen on the wall. The next patient is Mrs Cassidy. I sigh. I bet she's got something straight forward like a skin rash or an ear infection. I send another email.

Oi! Man of mystery, why are you ignoring all my messages? Hope I haven't hurt your tender feelings.

Again there's no reply. I look around the surgery. There are posters on the wall offering all kinds of help to victims of domestic violence, smokers, pregnant women, diabetics, women and men with breast cancer – I didn't know men got breast cancer – people with Parkinson's and how to spot the physical signs of someone who's suffered a stroke. No poster or leaflet offering *me* any advice or help or

167

support groups. I tune in to the tannoy and hear my name called. I look up and see it on the screen.

The next patient is Miss H Baldi

Room 15

I find my way to room 15, following the arrows. The door is shut. I knock and a friendly but professional voice invites me to enter. I push the door open so that I can't turn back and leave the surgery without seeing who is behind the door.

'Hello, come on in. I'm Doctor Khan. Sit down there. Now, what can I do for you?' It's a she. I didn't even ask the receptionist who the appointment would be with. I'm so glad it's a she.

'Um, I'm having a problem with my periods,' I say. I rehearsed a few sentences in my head while sitting in the waiting room but none of them feel right now I'm here.

'What kind of problems?' She's young, she's pretty and she has neat black hair caught in a ponytail. She's got small silver earrings, neutral-coloured lipstick and a bit of dark eyeliner. She's waiting for *me* to say something.

'I get problems the week before my period. I've just started using this app that tracks your menstrual cycle, it's called Clue.'

'I've heard good things about Clue and it's going to be really helpful that you've already got some data and information about your cycle. Well done,' she tells me without sounding patronising. She taps some information onto the screen. I want to know what she's writing about me but don't feel I can ask. The screen is turned slightly away from me. I wonder what her name is, she probably told me as I sat down but it's gone now.

'I read somewhere that caffeine makes things worse. I've made a list of all the things I've stopped eating and drinking.'

'It sounds like you have done the right thing, you've researched the impact food and drink can have on your body at certain times in your cycle. Good. Has this helped?' she asks.

I don't want her asking questions I can't answer. I want her to wave a magical medical wand and make this all better. Can't she just give me a prescription?

'It's getting worse if anything, but I don't think that's to do with food or drink. *I'm* getting worse,' I tell her.

'When you say *getting worse*, can you elaborate?'

Of course I can elaborate, I just don't want to.

'Moody,' I start, using the classic adjective but she puts her pen down, as if she knows this isn't what I mean. I wonder how long I've got in here before she gets fed up with me. I'm sure GP appointment slots aren't longer than ten minutes. I bet she's thinking, 'Come on! Get on with it, I haven't got all night!'

I breathe in air
and breathe out
Truth.

'I'm not depressed, this isn't depression, because the rest of the month I'm me again. It's just the one week. On that week I could spill some juice in the kitchen and it is the worst thing that's ever happened to me. Or someone at school could ask me for a crisp and I'll call them a disgusting, fat, greedy pig and I'll completely mean it. But I won't remember it. Or one of my friends might make a comment about what I'm wearing on a night out and I'll go from 0-100 on the anger scale and have to walk away from them so I don't do or say something really bad.' I stop talking for a second. She's listening to me, making notes on the screen, taking me seriously. So I carry on.

'I'll go and sit in a room on my own and people think I'm storming off for attention. I hear them say it after me, when my back is turned. The last thing I want is for someone to come and find me because it's not safe to be around me. I've wanted to tell someone all of this for ages but it sounds crazy. *I* sound crazy,' I confess. I'm not crying though. I thought I'd cry.

'How awful for you, just awful,' she says.

Great, *now* I'm crying.

'It sounds like you've been coping with this for quite a while?'

I nod because I can't find my voice. She passes me a box of tissues. I wonder how many boxes she gets through in a week.

'You've been very intelligent about this, emotionally and

physically. Your record keeping and awareness of your own body is hugely helpful, a big step in the right direction and a good way to begin to understand what you're going through. Now, what we're going to do...' she pauses and turns back to the screen to type something.

I let out a massive breath as I take in the 'we' in her sentence.

'...is start with some Fluoxetine, take one tablet every day for a month, then come back and see me. Keep using the app to make notes on how you are each day, what you've eaten and drunk, and note if and when the tablets start helping. If you can avoid alcohol as well as caffeine that might be wise. How does that sound?' she asks, as something prints out noisily in the corner of the room.

She collects the paper from the printer. 'Tablets don't work for everyone, or it can take a while to find the right tablets. There's two or three others we can try if we don't have any success with the Fluoxetine.' She keeps saying *we*. Things *we* can try, things *we* can do. I sit still, so still, and just listen to her friendly and professional voice. She's with me, it's her and me in this together. I could sit on this chair listening to her voice all night.

'And there's counselling and CBT, here's a leaflet which will explain it. If you decide you want to see a therapist, I can recommend Dr Dee, she has more expertise than me in this area. It is quite difficult to diagnose PMDD but it does sound as if this is what you are suffering from. Dr

171

Dee is a specialist in PMDD so we'll get you on her waiting list. Here's another leaflet which will explain PMDD a bit more and this leaflet – last one I promise – is a list of books on prescription, self-help guides. You should be able to get most of them at your local library.'

I want to hug her and kiss her and tell her all the things in my head but I don't. Instead I smile and take the prescription from her. I smile and shut the door behind me. I'm still smiling as I walk out of the surgery and into the pharmacy next door.

The chemist smiles back as I hand the prescription over. And I just can't stop smiling.

I'm not on my own anymore.

Relief wraps itself around me like a second skin as I put the white box with my name and address on in my bag.

We sit on faded red seats in the Swan theatre – Nonno's favourite. We're in the round, so close to the stage, behind a wooden balcony. We watch the cast bend, stretch, chat and sip from bottles of water. Behind them is an onstage wardrobe without doors. An array of ragged and well-worn costumes hang from hooks dangling from ropes which climb out of sight. Nonno waves to someone and they come over. I feel nervous. Nonno stands up, so I do too.

'Gianni! *Ciao! Come stai?' A* girl kisses Nonno on both cheeks.

'*Molto bene, grazie*, Lucia. This is my granddaughter, Hope. Hope, this is Lucia,' Nonno puts his arm about my shoulder.

'Hi,' I say, hoping that I'll have something more articulate to add. The girl – well, young woman really – has wide-apart green eyes that were smiling a second ago, but are now serious, taking me in. Her hair is a mess, black curls falling in her eyes. She needs some clean clothes, hers are covered in what looks like chalk. She's wearing a denim pinafore dress with a greying t-shirt which looks a size too small for her and loud stripy tights. Her black eyebrows dominate her face, which makes the green stand out all the more. She's stunning. I know she's just said something to me but I've no idea what. *Come on, Hope, think.* 'I'm Hope,' I tell her, which she of course already knows but she doesn't laugh.

'And I'm Lucia. Come, *come* and meet everyone.' She holds out her hand. It's warm and takes mine firmly. I thought I'd just be sitting with Nonno. I follow her on to one of the wooden walkways to the stage.

'Hey, everyone! This is Hope. Hope, this is everyone.' Lucia gestures to the people gathered on the stage, about eight, I think, not too intimidating. They're all women and girls, no boys or men, which feels *different*. Most of them smile or wave and say hi. I look out to the audience but the house lights are up so I can't see Nonno. I wonder if he's still there. Someone hands me a battered copy of *Top Girls*.

'We're on the kitchen scene with Joyce and Marlene,' another actress tells me, as if they don't mind me being on stage with them. 'Do you know the play?' I nod. 'Good, I'm Mae.' Then I place her: she's on the posters in the foyer. I'm sure I've seen her before, from something on the telly maybe. She looks a lot younger in real life, although she's probably got stage make-up on in the poster.

Someone sets two chairs out in the middle of the stage. There's already a table with two cups of tea. Mae and another woman head to the back of the stage, near the hanging costumes, I can't hear what they're saying. The rest of the women sit in a semi-circle facing the two chairs. I'm sat here, with them, on the RSC stage, about to watch their rehearsal.

'Right, are we ready? Vicky? Mae?' a woman calls out, I guess the director. The air changes and the lights dim. The faces of the two actors centre-stage transform. Mae's jaw drops down, making her lips jut out a bit. She draws her cheeks in, visibly souring. The other woman, who must be Vicky, rises in her chair a little, bringing her whole body into alignment – she becomes knowing and powerful. They start, their words shooting at one another.

I know this scene well. Aisha and Callie did it for their duologue. The best bit about it, apart from the swearing, was the way the two characters cut across each other naturally. All the other plays we'd read made sure that characters waited politely to speak their lines but this play threw all of that out the window. It felt more real, more honest. Lucia is standing at a funny angle, like she's waiting to join the scene. I take in her clothes again and realise she must be playing the kid, Angie. That explains her odd fashion choices, she's in costume. Mae and Vicky pause, then move to the director – I wish I knew her name. I turn to hear them better.

'…it's the brutality of the honesty, though, that's what we want to see,' Vicky replies to whatever the director just said. 'They say things to each other that they'd never say to anyone else. They know how to hurt with their words because they're family.'

I think about Mum and me and all the ways I've hurt her with my words.

'Yes, this, *this*, and also the undertones of the lost child. Joyce is dripping with pent-up resentment about all the sacrifices she's made,' Mae adds.

I think about what Mum said, about needing to do something for herself for once. I picture all the sacrifices she's made for me.

'And the play asks us, the audience, does Marlene's behaviour – to become the kind of woman she wants to be – excuse her? Can we forgive her the mistakes?' the director asks.

I wonder if Mum will be able to forgive me for saying I hated her.

'It's all about choices. What has to be sacrificed. You can't have everything, or at least not without some repercussions!' Vicky declares.

I can't imagine having a child. I don't know whether I want kids. I can't see my body working well enough to make a baby – a lot of the time it struggles to get through the day without a complete breakdown.

'And Marlene makes the ultimate sacrifice when she

hands over her child. She's made to pay!' Mae says – and, before I can stop myself, I'm responding too.

'But both of them make huge sacrifices, not *just* Marlene,' I say. I only know I've said it out loud because everyone turns to look at me. I was keeping all my other thoughts in my head, but this one escaped.

'Yeah, you're right. They're both deeply flawed.' Mae nods. She's thinking about what *I've* said, really considering it.

'All of them are. All of us are, we're all deeply flawed, that's what makes us so interesting,' the director adds, and they laugh and I join in. I *get* it, the truth of it.

'That's what's universal about this play. No matter your gender you can relate to the characters. They make mistakes and then have to try to fix them,' Lucia adds, to me. I worry that Nonno's said something about me and my situation. She's sat cross-legged on the floor, looking encouragingly at me.

'I think Churchill's maybe saying you can't escape your past even when you're powerful, like Marlene?' I can't stop my voice going up at the end, as if I'm unsure. 'Even if you're an adult and you've got all the power, you still can't run and hide,' I add.

We discussed this loads in Theatre Studies but this isn't a safe little lesson. This play is on this stage in The Swan theatre and people out there, like me, are going to pay to see it. They're going to go online and pick seats and maybe book a table for a meal after. And they'll watch these women, then they'll go home and talk about it. But do I *want* this, to be one of the actors people go home and talk about? I don't know how I'd feel about that, strangers discussing my voice, my body, the way I said certain lines, or the way my face looked. I know I like being part of the debate but that's very different from standing in a place like this, with people like them, in front of a real audience of strangers who don't know me and don't care about me.

'Power is key. Take the scene with Angie and Kit for example,' Vicky says, and they all start talking over one another – just like Joyce and Marlene.

'Good, good. Mae, Vicky, I think we'll move forwards to Marlene's line: "You were quick enough to take her," Alright?' the director says. Someone switches the teacups for glasses of apple juice. Mae and Vicky walk back to the chairs and their body language changes again. Vicky is leaning forwards now, possessive and assured, whiskey glass in hand. She looks confrontational but animal-like, too, as if she's eyeing up her prey.

I know this scene, I've watched Callie do it enough times. Mae is poised like she's ready for a fight. The air is tight and the rest of us feel it, wired and rigid. It's almost unpleasant, too close, too fraught, but I find myself inching closer. I'm swimming in every single drop of the tension. The first grenade is yet to be thrown but you can see what's to come just by looking at them, you can see the warfare that's about to take place.

'And then what happened?' Nonno asks. He's barely touched his panini, but I don't have time to ask him why he's not hungry. I've got too much to say. We're sat on benches by the river Avon and I'm shovelling food and drink in as fast as I can because we've been asked to stay and watch tonight's press performance. Nonno couldn't buy any tickets, they'd sold out, but Susannah – I finally learned the director's name – invited us to stay and watch. They always keep a seat or two spare on press night and tonight we're the lucky ones.

'Yes, Lucia asked Susannah if it'd be alright, which was really kind of her. I think I was supposed to just be watching but when Susannah found out I knew the play she let me join in!'

'So you were Angie!' I can sense his excitement. He understands what this means to me.

'Yes! I had Lucia's spare costume and she lent me her script. Susannah asked me questions about Angie and gave me some notes and Vicky and Mae were really patient. We ran the scene several times. I could have done it all day long. Susannah said that my projection is really strong,' I tell him, trying hard not to sound like someone with a crush. I must have mentioned her name at least ten times so far, but she is the director after all.

'Did Lucia give you any advice?' Nonno asks. I shake my head.

'No, she let me take it. She just sat back and watched. I think she didn't want me to feel like I had to copy her Angie, so she let me find my own version. But she told me afterwards that … that Susannah said I wasn't bad,' I say shyly.

'Ha! Praise indeed, *piccolina*. And how did it feel, this being *not bad*?' He gets to the heart of the matter, cracking open his sparkling water. He pops a tablet out of a packet and swallows it.

'Have you got a headache?' I ask him. It's pretty hot in the sun. He nods and sips more water, then waves his hand and points back to the theatre, telling me to carry on talking, so I do. I can't not. 'Nonno, I feel lit up.' I tell him honestly.

'Ah, I *see*,' he says.

'What?' I ask.

'You know there isn't an open door here? We have to go home tonight, back into the world. I've spoken to your *mamma*. She's not happy. I will explain it better to her in person. Don't worry. Hope, this is just a taste, *si*? Just to show you what can be. The rest is up to you. You have to go out and find your own door.' He stands and puts his rubbish in the bin. 'And now, we must go. Susannah is expecting you!' he says with a smile. I smile back, because he's right, the rest *is* up to me, it's my choice.

I rush into Waterstones and look around for Callie. She's standing at a table of books holding two already. I spot a Foyles carrier bag on the floor next to her, she's obviously had a good shopping session in the station, she must have caught an early train from Shrewsbury. I watch her before she's seen me – she looks relaxed, holidayed and happy. As if she senses me, she looks up, drops both books back and runs to me.

'Congratulations!' I hold out my arms to her.

'I know, right? I was starting to think I might not get in anywhere,' she laughs with the ease of someone who's safe. 'You know the theatre school's around the corner from your hospital?' Of course, I know where it is. While I'm stuck in hospital, she'll be starting at Birmingham Theatre School.

'So, how was the holiday?' I change the subject.

'A-MAZE-ING. Total blast. But I missed you a

disgusting amount,' she says into my hair. We part and she carries on. 'There was loads of street theatre and singing in the evenings, which you'd have loved. I wish you'd come with us. They even had snow globes there! I got you one, total cheese-fest with glitter and plastic figurines.'

I remember the awkward moment her parents asked if I wanted to come with them. Even if we'd had money for the flight I couldn't have left Mum. It wouldn't have been fair – but now, looking at Callie, I kind of wish I had.

'How was Ethan? Did you get to skip the queue again?' I ask.

'You're not going to believe this but he was fine this time. We went through a different entrance from everyone else. Mum organised it with the airport first. Dad bought Ethan's ear defenders and his blanket. It all worked, especially the stuff I downloaded for him on to his iPad. So, have you heard from *him* yet?' She doesn't need to say his name.

I shake my head. 'Did you make Ethan a social storybook again?' I ask, avoiding the subject.

'Yeah, Mum made one this time. It had photos of the villa and his bedroom there, the toys he could take with him, the pool, the plane, both airports. She even did a "how many sleeps" count down in the book. The owners were lovely and sent their own photos of the garden which weren't on the website so Ethan could picture it all before we got there. Their granddaughter is autistic so they were really helpful,' Callie explains. It had been her idea to make a photo-book for Ethan when they moved house a few years ago. 'Anyway, Miss Sidestep-the-question, why haven't you heard from Riley?'

'Dunno. It's been two weeks now and nothing,' I tell her.

'Have you sent more emails or texts?'

I nod.

'Tell you what, if karma doesn't get him I will. You shouldn't have asked him to meet you. It was too soon,' Callie tells me as we walk through the adult fiction section and head up the stairs to the YA department.

'Don't you think I know that?' I rush up the stairs.

'All right! Calm down, don't take it out on *me...*' she replies, catching me up.

'I'm not, it's just when you say stuff like that... I don't need to hear it!' I try and calm down but it isn't easy. It happens so quickly, the flaring up and the volume and the anger.

'*Alright*, take it easy.' She shakes her hair out – she must have had it relaxed: the box braids have been replaced by a sleek short bob. She puts on a smile and starts chatting, as if we were in the middle of a perfectly lovely conversation, neatly negotiating the edges of an argument. 'So where were you last night? I called round as soon as we got back with your snow globe but your mum said you were out, with Nonno.'

'Oh, he took me to Stratford for the day,' I tell her carefully, although I'm not sure why I'm being cagey. I should tell her it was my idea.

'Ah, he's so lush, isn't he? Wish my grandfather was more like him. So, what did you see?' she asks, putting down another book.

'*Top Girls.*'

'Oh, that's *my* play! I could have come!' she whines.

'Two weeks in a French villa not enough for you?' skips out of my mouth before I can get a handle on it.

'I didn't mean it like that. I just meant it could have been fun to come too. And I asked you to come with us on holiday,' she reminds me.

'I know, I know. Sorry, ignore me,' I apologise. 'Anyway, it was a last-minute thing.'

'So, what was it like? Good cast?' Callie asks.

'Incredible. All-female cast and crew. I think Lucia was the best, she played Angie in such a unique way, really focusing on her proximity to other characters by invading their personal space. Susannah, that's the director, was so clever, the way she'd get them to deliver a line completely differently in rehearsal so that it changed the meaning of the scene every time.' I can't stop now I've started. 'Susannah told me she wanted the set to be minimalist with costumes hanging down and just a table and chairs because...'

'Hang on, how do *you* know this Susannah director woman? Did you get to go backstage? Who's Lucia?' Callie interrupts, saying their names like I've cheated on her. 'Hope?' She grabs my arm.

'I did a bit of a workshop with them. Well, I got to watch them rehearse,' I tell her.

She looks hurt, jealous, cross and then something else, her face changing frame by frame.

'I was going to tell you,' I add in quickly. 'It all happened at the last minute.'

'Yeah, so you said.' She takes her arm away from mine. 'This book looks good,' she says, picking up the first book she can lay her hands on.

'Cal, I was going to tell you.' I reach out to touch her but she moves on to the next table.

'I've been wanting to read this for ages,' she tells me, practically shoving a book into my hands. I look down at it. 'It's a Malorie Blackman, so you know it's going to be good. You should get it, Hope. It's about *Othello*.' She's talking and talking and talking, not letting me explain.

'I remember it. Jealousy, right?' I challenge.

'Yeah, right. So, *the* RSC, hey?' she sighs. 'Lucky you.'

'Yes, *the* RSC.' I put the book back on the table.

'Some people get all the luck,' she says under her breath, with just enough volume for me to hear her.

'Are you serious, Callie? Are you mad? I mean, look at you! Swanning off to your French villa with your perfect family before you start your real life, the life you want, the life *I* want. I get fuck all luck!' I tell her hard. I tell her loud. I tell her the truth because right now she can't see it.

'*God*, I didn't mean it like that. Just y'know, you're

185

connected. Your Nonno's got connections. I wish I had someone like him in my life, that's all.'

'He's hardly *connected*. He just knew someone whose granddaughter was in the cast. I asked him to ask her for a favour, okay? It was my idea, not Nonno's. There's no such thing as luck, you have to make stuff happen,' I tell her. She's living in a fairy tale. 'And anyway, you weren't even in the country, so I couldn't have asked you to come, could I?'

I'm shouting and I don't care. I'm making my own scene right now, directing, writing, producing and starring in it, and we're beginning to gather a very British audience of browsers pretending not to eavesdrop on our row.

'You want to know the truth? The holiday was boring, alright? Happy now? I sat about by the pool and read all my books and listened to Ethan telling me how air-conditioning units work and what the chances of the plane crashing on the way home are. Mum and Dad pretty much argued on and off the whole time about re-mortgaging the house. Oh and the best part was it rained. For a whole week, so much for sunny south of France. And if you'd been there, instead of hobnobbing with your connections at the RSC, it would have all been okay! I wouldn't have given a crap about the rain!' Now she's loud too. Our audience is growing.

'Well, you didn't say that, did you? How was I to know? And don't be stupid, we might be Italian but we're not in

186

with the mafia, okay? *Connections*, grow up, Callie! It was just a rehearsal. It's not like it's going to lead anywhere. It was just one random day. And if you'd been here I would have asked you to come with me,' I tell her, secretly glad I didn't have to make that choice.

'Really?' she asks, hope in her eyes.

'Really. And you'll always be *my* Marlene,' I add to make her laugh. And it works.

The audience disperses, returning to the blurbs on the books they've been holding all this time.

'So, I'm going to wander. Meet you in the coffee shop in ten?' she asks me. Just like that, it's over for her. She knows it was just one day and it meant nothing. I'm not going to be given the keys to the RSC stage door.

'Alright. See you in ten,' I agree, relieved to have a bit of time and space apart. I look at Callie to check she's really fine, but she's already on the floor reading, escaping easily into someone else's world.

I spot a small section tucked away in the corner: the self-help zone. I skim the shelves, over a lot of parenting guides: *The Terrible Twos, The Tricky Tweens, The Turbulent Teens* and *Eat Yourself Thin* and *Think Yourself Slim*. There's lots on psychology. It has a whole subsection on depression, which is brilliant for those who are depressed, but I need something different and I can't find it. It seems like no one knows about this period problem, apart from way too many people on the internet. I need a book on PMDD, a chunky book, full of references and bibliographies and contents and indexes and help.

'Can I help you?' a member of staff asks. I freeze. I try to say no but my head goes up and down, and then I stare at her, in silence, for way too long.

'What are you looking for? Do you know the author?'

I shrug. Why am I not talking? Yes, there's something I'm looking for, but I can't seem to say it to her.

'There aren't any books on it. It's fine, I'll find something online,' I tell her finally.

'Are you sure? I could look it up on our system if you like?' She points to the cash desk and the computer. I smile and follow her across the shop. She has curly red hair and a huge gap between her front teeth. Her tongue is pierced and for a second I can't take my eyes off it.

'I said, do you know the title?' I shake my head. She laughs. 'How about the colour?' She's trying hard. This is the part where I'm supposed to talk. I clear my throat.

'No, sorry. It's about PMDD. Don't worry, you won't find anything, I don't think. I don't want to waste your time.'

She smiles, silver bracelets clanking. She starts typing into her search engine, frowning.

'Nope, you're right, nothing coming up. I'll do a search, what does PDMM stand for?'

'It's PMDD not PDMM. Look, it doesn't matter. I've got to get back to work.'

She looks disappointed. 'If you find the title you're

looking for, come back and I'll order it in for you,' she offers. But she can't help me because there's a gap on the shelf.

'We're going to make a Hope Chest,' I announce, sitting cross-legged on my bedroom floor. Callie sits opposite me.

'What's a Hope Chest? Did you make it up?' she asks.

I check my phone to see if Riley's texted which he hasn't, which is fine. It's Saturday night. THE going-out night, so he's probably out somewhere in Dublin, having a life, doing IT and hasn't noticed all my messages. Messages that I shouldn't have sent, *maybe*.

'Hope, what's this chest thingy?' Callie interrupts.

I close my email and open a tab with Google.

'Alright, Ms Otis, a Hope Chest was a well-known custom for women before they got married,' I read out loud. She looks unimpressed, so I carry on. 'What goes into a Hope Chest, I hear you ask? I've got it here somewhere.' I scroll through my phone looking for more information.

'But, Hope, I'm not getting married, not now and not ever, so why do I need a Hope box? You don't have to do this. We're fine. We're *us.*' She thinks this is a making-up evening. She thinks I'm still worried about our row, and about everything that's been going wrong between us since Dublin, since before Dublin.

'Well, yes, I know we're *us*, but you still need a Hope Chest. We're going to put loads of our things in it, so that when you go off to drama col – when you *go*, you've got things that will remind you of us. I might make Ethan one too, if you think that'd be alright with your mum?' I offer.

'Sure. I'm only going to Birmingham, Hope,' she states the obvious. But this isn't about geography. It just matters that *she's* going. I shrug, so she switches subjects.

'So, how is that man-boy who's stalking you via text? You haven't mentioned him in days now? I feel like I need an omnibus edition to catch up.' Callie waits for an answer. 'Pop open those Pringles then.' She hands them over and I rip the lid off. But I don't have an omnibus edition of Riley-related gossip for her. There's not even a single episode. It might not have helped that I suggested he was brainless in our last exchange. Sounds slightly offensive now, looking back. And then there's the last message I sent, that might have been a huge mistake.

'I thought we could put in this photo of us when we started in Year 7, and those friendship bracelets we made each other in Year 8, which stink by the way. You also have to put in some linen so I've cut the badge off my blazer. *Is* that linen? Just to be safe, we could put in that crocheted blanket we made at Guides or we could cut a bit off it. And we have to put one of our snow globes in, but only one. We could cut off locks of our hair – what even are locks? Is that like a whole chunk or just a few strands? Sounds like something from a Shakespeare play! Or we could do the whole *Blood Brothers* thing. Remember when we went to see it in Year 10?' I look around my room for something sharp. I'm aware it's unravelling, the panic inside me at the thought of her going, leaving me here, but I can't reign it in.

'Slow down! What are you looking for? *A knife*?' she laughs nervously. 'Do you keep knives up here?' I can hear she's serious. She's really asking me that.

'*Cal*! Course I haven't got a knife. I was kidding about the *Blood Brothers* thing. Why would I have a knife in my room? What are you saying?' She thinks I've got a knife up here. That I've been hurting myself? Cutting myself?

'Calm down, I just wondered if…' She can't finish her sentence and for once I'm glad. I don't need to hear it. I can see it on her face.

'No! No, I do not nor have I ever had a knife in my room. What is the matter with you?'

She looks pained. 'I don't know. This was meant to be a nice evening. Look, I've brought Pringles and Haribos. I thought that we might be able to talk, you know, really talk…' She's lost. Pryia is right, I can't leave this any longer.

'Cal, you're right. We do need to talk. I need to tell you something.'

She looks scared. 'Hope, *wait*, you don't have to,' she starts to backtrack. 'I didn't mean to push you.' I can see she isn't ready yet, but *I* am. It has to be now. Or she'll go off to drama college and it'll become THE THING I haven't told her. She's the only person on the planet I can be my whole self with, so I can't keep lying to her. It's too hard and it's not fair.

'I've got this thing. I'm ill but not like dying ill and I can get help.' I am talking too fast. I walk around my room, moving papers about on my desk, straightening my duvet which doesn't need straightening, until the noise she's making stops my pacing. Callie is crying. She never cries because she's not a pretty crier.

'Oh, Cal, please don't cry. It's fine. I'll be fine. I promise.' I wrap my arms around her, but I keep talking because if I don't get this out now I never will.

'I didn't mean to scare you. I've got PMDD. It's like PMS's big bad ugly sister. They can fix it.' I stop because there's no way she can keep her questions in.

'You promise, it's not terminal or life-threatening? How do you know they can fix it?' she croaks. 'I knew there was something wrong with you! Why didn't you just tell me?' she demands. 'I've been imagining all kinds of hideous things!'

'There's nothing *wrong* with me! Look, there's this woman at the hospital who has it and she gave me a leaflet and she's right. She's right.' It sinks in even more as I say it out loud.

'But why didn't you tell *me*? I mean, why are you telling a complete stranger, some random woman at the hospital about your periods? Why are you telling *her* first?' she whispers. She doesn't sound like the Callie I know; she sounds afraid.

'I didn't know I had it. I didn't know what it was. She worked it out because she's got it too.'

'I've been asking you for months, so basically you've been lying to me all this time?'

'No! How could I lie about something I'd never even heard of?'

'I knew you weren't right! We could have worked it out together. We could have found out what was wrong with you,' she keeps on. 'I'm your best friend, that's what I'm here for,' she says angrily, as if I need reminding.

'You've already listened to me go on and on about Dad. I've already told you every single sad thought in my head. I've used up all my best friend late-night phone calls and I didn't want to lay any more stress or grief on you, Cal.'

She doesn't reply.

'There's only so much a person can deal with. I thought if I leaned on you anymore you might break.' I tell her the truth. I've leaned on her more than anyone else, over and over.

'Are you really that stupid, Hope? Don't you know, there's no limit?' She stops, as if she doesn't know what to say next or is too furious to say it.

I sit there, holding the tube of Pringles, and wonder what to do to make this right.

'After everything we've been through, how can you think like that? It's not like there's a time-up on friendship. If you can't tell me about stuff like this, then what's the fucking point of *us*? What's the point of you and me? You might as well be best friends with hospital girl or the new love of your life, Susannah the RSC director person!' She's so angry with me, as if these people could replace her, or even come close. I don't know what to say. She's never spoken to me like this before. I've never hurt her like this before.

'Hope, you're my best friend.'

I forget how to breathe.

'Part of the job description is dealing with all the shitty stuff as well as cupcakes and sleepovers. You can't pick and choose and just skip to the good bits.' She's really telling me off now but I let her.

'I'm sorry, Cal, I shouldn't have hidden all this stuff from you,' I start to apologise, but she cuts in, she won't let me fix things.

'Seriously, it's not as if you need to protect *me*. I mean, I *can* cope, Hope! I can handle this PMS stuff,' she protests and I'd normally believe her. But now it's like we've traded places and we're trying out for the parts of each other for the very first time.

As if she senses the seesaw of our friendship tip the wrong way, she jumps up and reverses the roles, so everything is back where it should be. 'Now, turn on the laptop and let's work out what this PMD thingy is and how we can fix it,' Callie declares, viciously flipping open the lid to my laptop before I can stop her. I jump across the room ready to slam the lid down but I'm too slow. She's already seen what's on the screen.

'What the actual... *Tell* me you haven't sent this yet?' Callie splutters, spinning round to look at me.

The last email on the screen is the one I sent to Riley, three days ago.

'What if he says yes? Has he said yes? Just how many secrets are you keeping?' she asks, and before I can come up with an excuse, she adds, 'I feel like I don't know you anymore, Hope.' Which feels like the very worst thing anyone has ever said to me.

'I thought you said I should meet him. I was only taking your advice.'

'I did not! I mean, yeah, maybe, but not like this! I meant properly. *This is not safe!* Do you not watch the news? Have you forgotten all those internet safety days at school?' she shouts. I shush her, not wanting Mum or worse still Nonno to come charging in. 'You don't even know this guy!' she starts up again. 'He's some random dude. You can't trust him. You don't even know what he wants from you,' she adds darkly.

'I do trust him and we do know each other! He saved me.'

She rolls her eyes at me. 'What are you on about? *No!* You and I know each other. You and he do NOT know each other. What do *you* need saving from?'

This is too much, too much information coming out too quickly.

'Myself,' I tell her, unable to keep the drama out of my voice. But this is real. This isn't a made-up life on the stage, words written on a script. This is me inside and out. I have to tell her how I met Riley on the ferry even if it means this mess it too big to fix and that I've broken *us*.

'And what did he say? Is he going to meet you?' she asks, after ten minutes of serious silence.

'He hasn't replied yet. Maybe he's busy?'

'I thought you said he texts you every day?' she snaps.

'He does usually. He used to, anyway. Maybe he's lost his phone or something. That's why I emailed him as well.'

'Uh huh,' she grunts, sounding less than convinced, which puts me on edge. I check my phone again to see if there's anything from him. No.

'Maybe you've scared him off? Been a bit stalker-ish with all the texts and emails?' She says what I can't, what I don't want to face.

'He started the whole thing. He asked to meet up first!' I've had enough of the heart to heart. The last thing I need to hear is that I might have sent Riley running.

'Don't snap at me, don't you dare snap at me. Everyone knows long-distance relationships don't work. I've tried to tell you that,' Callie lectures.

'Have you had one – a long-distance relationship? How do *you* know?' Callie doesn't do relationships. She's focusing on her career first and isn't going to waste her time on small-town boys.

'No, but…' She pulls her 'trust me I know what I'm doing' face.

I sigh. If he doesn't want to meet, I'm not going to have a breakdown, and I can see that's what she's worried about, now she knows. I knew this would happen once I told her about PMDD. She's looking at me like I've got a special snowflake label stuck on my forehead. I'm different from her now. This is why I held off from telling her. This is why I'll now be Hope but with added PMDD and any little thing that goes wrong will now be linked to this. Even if she doesn't say it out loud, she'll be thinking it. I feel betrayed.

'And even if you do meet, what then? He'll break your heart. He sounds like a right tart from what you've told me!' she carries on. I immediately regret showing her any of his flirty messages. 'I mean, do you really want your sexual debut to be with someone like this?' I wince at the phrase *sexual debut* and wish she wasn't quite so theatre about it all.

'I don't see what the big deal is; felt like the next step to me,' I huff.

'Stop being so naïve, Hope. Listen to this… "Hi Mum and Nonno, on the way back from Dublin I met this boy who stopped me from… I don't know what? Jumping overboard because I didn't get in to drama college?"'

'Oh, don't be ridiculous. I wasn't going to jump overboard!' I wish I'd never told her. 'I was standing on the rail because, because I just wanted to get away from myself. And he made me wobble by grabbing my jacket. I was fine until he came along!'

She's not listening. 'Oh and here's the kicker: I've also got PMDT which controls my moods and makes me do irrational things like climbing up safety rails on ferries to scream at the sea.' She pauses to leave me with that image. 'Anyway, back to the strange man-child on the ferry who smokes dope. Well, he gave me his number, except he secretly hacked into my email account and since then we've been messaging, chatting and generally having great big sexy relations under your nose.'

'We haven't been having sexy relations. We haven't been having sexy *anything*, Callie!'

It's no good. She's raging.

'It's alright if I go and meet him on my own and not tell anyone where I'm going, isn't it? We're just gonna find a hotel room somewhere and Netflix and chill?'

'No one even mentioned a hotel room, stop being so ridiculous.' I have visions of Mum thundering up the stairs to see what's going on.

'Oh and, before I go off to meet this potential paedophile who I've met all of once, we'd better revisit the PMMT thingy, which is an illness which makes me really angry and aggressive and behave in a way I'd never normally. REPEAT it makes me behave in a way that I would *NEVER* normally.' Callie is on her feet now, doing a scarily good impression of me.

She turns round and looks at me with an expression I don't recognise, then asks, '*Who are you?*' which crushes me.

When I don't answer she yells, 'And you can keep your pathetic Hope Chest!' She storms out of my room.

'Come *back*, Callie?' I plead but it's too late. She's stomping down the stairs. For a hideous second I think she's going to tell Mum and Nonno. A tiny part of me wishes she would, just to get it over in one go, then they can all hate me together. I feel sick as I hover on the landing, listening to her lying to them, saying that she's feeling unwell and would Mum mind driving her home? Nonno says something quietly to her and she answers. I can't hear them properly. Maybe Callie's asking Nonno to take her to the RSC.

There's no point going down there to try and talk her out of leaving, so I go back into my room. I sit on my bed and think about her last question. Her words wound, just as they were meant to. She doesn't get it. I just know nothing bad will happen to me if I meet Riley. I can't explain it to her because I can hear how dodgy it sounds, how dangerous. I think I'd know if he was someone to be scared of. But if she'd suggested the same thing, I'd absolutely tell her not to do it. We've had enough lectures at school and college on internet safety and grooming, but this isn't what's been going on between Riley and me. We have met! He isn't a stranger luring me in. He isn't an older man pretending to be a young boy and he isn't an axe murderer after my blood. The truth is he's barely interested in me at all. The scariest thing about him is the fact that I sent that email days ago and he still hasn't replied.

When we get back home, we search in the dark for a parking space. As soon as Mum has finished straightening up the car, I jump out. I open the front door. Scout starts barking and rushes out of the kitchen to greet us, her massive tail crashing into my legs. I sit on the mat and pull her onto my lap as Nonno and Mum step around me and head into the kitchen. There's post on the mat, underneath Scout. I pull out a scary-looking brown envelope with my name on. I push Scout off my lap, brush black and white dog hair off me, and walk into the kitchen, her damp nose pressed against the back of my calf, giving me a thorough sniffing. I put the brown envelope on the table.

'What's that? Aren't you going to open it?' Mum says, pouring herself a glass of red wine. She doesn't offer Nonno one.

'My results.'

Nonno switches on the coffee machine and holds an espresso cup out to me in question. I shake my head. I probably could risk a coffee but I'm not going to. The doctor told me if I can live without caffeine and avoid alcohol the tablets will work better. Whatever it takes.

I tear it open. I look at the first page, then the second, and then all the other sheets, taking in each result. Mum puts down her wine.

'So, how did you do?' she asks.

'Not good.'

'Put us out of our misery?' she pleads. 'It's been a very long night already.' She looks pointedly at Nonno. 'The last thing you should be having at this hour is an espresso,' she tells him. He ignores her.

'A* for Music, A for French, B for English Lit, C for English Lang, C for Maths, double C for Science, D for Humanities, an E for Tech. And a B for Drama.' I look up to see her rearrange her face. She looks strangely relieved.

'But that's brilliant. You've done brilliantly!' She grabs me and kisses me, hugs me then kisses me again, holding my face in her hands. I pull away and she looks hurt.

'Mum, they're rubbish results, all over the place!' My voice comes out squashed. 'I was predicted A*s and Bs not Ds and Es. *I* got a B for Drama! A pathetic B, for God's sake!' I shout.

'I know you were expecting an A and...'

'I was predicted an A*.'

'An A* then. At least you got one for Music, that's brilliant and…'

'I can't believe you're using words like brilliant!'

'You know, just because I don't agree with your grandfather and this ridiculous RSC trip on your secret day out to Stratford, it does not make me a bad person!' she snaps. 'I am not the enemy here. I never told you you'd get an A*.'

'I didn't say you did. And who said anything about Stratford or the RSC? I wasn't even talking about acting.'

'For once,' Mum murmurs, but I hear her.

'*God*, I just wish…' I stop myself.

'No, do go on, what do you wish, Hope?' She picks up her wine to take a sip.

'Just that you'd be a bit more like Nonno, and do stuff, help me make decisions and come up with choices,' I say, knowing she's not going to want to hear it. Before she can respond Nonno comes back into the room.

'*Scusa*, I bought this when you were born, *piccolina*. Is it a good time to open it now?' he says, before kissing me on both cheeks. Mum shrugs. 'A peace offering, Erin? It is time to celebrate the good that has happened?' he suggests.

'Really? Alcohol, Gianni?' Mum reprimands, before she snatches three champagne flutes from the wedding cupboard that's only opened on very special occasions. She slams them down on the little table so hard I'm surprised they don't shatter.

I panic. This is not a special occasion and I don't want the champagne Nonno is pouring out shakily into the glasses. One glass might wreck my medication. How am I going to say no to Nonno's special champagne? I can't think of a good reason. The champagne spills over. Mum tuts then mops it up. Nonno hands out the glasses and opens his mouth to make a speech, to toast me and say things about me that just aren't true. I have to stop him.

'I don't know why you're making such a fuss. I haven't done anything worth all this, have I, Mum? *You've* made that clear. You think I'm a complete failure, don't you, Mum? Just a fucking failure!' The panic rises up and fizzes out of me.

'That is it! I have had enough. You do not get to speak to me like that. I don't deserve it. Go to your room!' she spits.

Nonno winces.

'Are you serious?' I say half-laughing.

'*Go!* she shouts. 'Just get out!' She can't stand the sight of me right now.

I do as she says, glad of a reason to leave the room, the brown envelope and her.

'I don't think you're going to be able to sing today…' a nurse starts as Pryia and I walk into Kofi's room and I feel deflated. I played Tracy Chapman all night, memorising the new lyrics to 'Give Me One Reason' I'd written just for him. It also took my mind off the stupid row with Mum. And the one with Callie.

'They've got to. Oh, yes, yes. He'll need distracting if they're going to do this,' Kofi's mum interrupts. Her son is hidden, enclosed by white coats and important voices. The room is full of people all crowded around his bed.

'What are they doing to him?' I ask, earning a sharp look from Pryia.

'Lumbar puncture,' his mum tells me, clearly not remotely bothered about sharing information. I don't know what a lumbar puncture is or even *where* your lumbar is, but it sounds painful. Puncturing anything isn't good, especially a small body like his. The nurse and Pryia exchange a quick look and then the nurse nods, giving us permission.

'Stay there until they get started and then stand over there. They'll need room to work,' she instructs, looking as unsure about this as I am. This does not look like the time to be singing but his mum is insistent. I want to move across to the bed, push the gowned ghosts out of the way and see Kofi for myself, check he's actually in there and hasn't somehow disappeared in his Tardis. I want to see his face, to make him smile, but I do as I am told and stay away from all the doctors clustered around his bed.

'Keep your back arched like that, good boy. Mum, perhaps if you could come here, this side please, and hold Kofi's hand?' the anaesthetist says. Kofi's mum – I don't know her name, walks around the bed, people move out of the way, and finally I catch a glimpse of Kofi's hair. He has white sheets over him but his back is exposed. I see a needle like nothing I've ever seen before: it looks inhumane. If that thing is going in his back, it is going to hurt more than anyone in the room can begin to imagine. Pryia takes my hand and holds it tightly. We shuffle over to Kofi's mum, trying very hard not to get in the way.

'Please sing to him?' she begs us, looking at me. 'He needs you to sing to him, Hope.' I didn't even know she knew my name.

'Of course.'

Kofi's eyes are on the three of us. He looks completely terrified, which makes me feel scared too.

'Shall we sing our song about space again?' Pryia asks Kofi, but he shakes his head. I'm finding it difficult to know where to look. There's a team of people behind him preparing stuff which I can't see because Kofi's body is in the way. I settle on looking at Kofi's curly hair, soft and short, as if he's just had it clipped. I want to stroke it and so I do, looking at his mum first. She nods her permission for me to touch him.

'What do you want us to sing, Kofi?' I whisper, stroking his hair, but he won't answer me, he won't even look at me. 'Kofi, how about some more Tracy Chapman?' I ask, and finally he turns his head, gives me a tiny nod and then closes his eyes. His mum mouths *thank you* to me.

'But I don't know any Tracy Chapman off by heart,' Pryia blurts out. She sounds panicked.

'Don't worry, I do.'

Kofi's mum keeps holding his hand, tears sliding down her face, as I sing the first line from 'Give Me One Reason'. Pryia recognises the chorus and joins in with relief. I don't look at the doctors, I don't look at all their sterile equipment or their gowns and gloves. I shut them all out and focus on him. And then I sing his song, the one I wrote just for him.

Kofi's Song

I know one reason to stay here
And it'll change your mind
Stop worrying your lovely *Mamma*
Come on Kofi now be kind
There's worlds out there for you to explore
See what your sonic screwdriver can find

Aliens full of guts and gore
A *Dr Who* fan couldn't want more
How about a trip in the Tardis
with Oswin?
That'd be bliss
Kofi get better, please try
And get better
I know you know you got this.

Give you one reason to stay here?
How about a Big Mac for lunch?
Or maybe a caramel McFlurry dear?
Oh, I got your number there.
I know you don't wanna leave me lonely
And this song's gonna change your mind.

When I look up the room is almost empty. All the doctors, anaesthetists and consultants have left. There are only two nurses monitoring Kofi. I wonder when they all went. The room was so full and noisy.

It is silent, apart from the beeps of Kofi's machine. Kofi is asleep. His mum is still holding his hand. Pryia looks at me and without speaking we leave the room as quietly as we can.

Outside, I can think again. I feel like I've fallen back into the real world. The doors open and close behind us, as people walk in off Steel House Lane and out again. Taxis arrive and drop people off, buses hiss past and cars search for a parking space. It all carries on. There's a few parents outside smoking, guilty hooded looks cross their faces as they notice us in what looks like a hospital uniform. Pryia and I head down the road.

'How did you know he liked Tracy Chapman?' she asks, taking a Mars bar out of her pocket, opening it and bending it into two equal pieces.

'He told me.' I take my half gratefully. I need a sugar boost, even though my body is supposed to be a temple now.

'Your voice is … so *rare*. I know I keep on about it, sorry, but … it's like velvet.' I can hear something in her voice, admiration and maybe a bit of jealousy. 'Are you going to come to choir rehearsals now? There's still time for you to

211

sing with us in the concert. I know you won't have had long to rehearse but we could do with your voice. And those song-writing skills!'

I laugh.

'So? Going to join us?'

'Yes,' I decide. After singing to Kofi the decision is easy.

'We'll be in the church this week. We're going to sing by candlelight, like we will on the night of the concert. Just you wait, Hope, there's nothing like the Singing Medicine choir.' Pryia smiles.

Singing to Kofi feels different. It isn't like singing passionate lyrics about the French Revolution when I joined Shropshire Youth Theatre and we did *Les Mis*, or the heightened drama when I sang in Carmen with the junior operatic society. Or singing about how much Bill Sykes needs me when I was Nancy in *Oliver!* This is intimate and authentic and I want to do it more. It helped; I could see it helped him and his mum. I want to sit by his bedside and sing all day long, as high and as low as I can go and distract him and his mum all I can. I want to go back in, but Pryia keeps on walking away from the hospital. I think if she could she'd break into a run right now.

'Pryia, stupid question, but are you alright?'

She shakes her head. 'I've never seen a lumbar puncture before. I know it's to do with infection, obviously, but I wonder what they're testing for.' She sounds so unsure.

'Maybe his mum will tell us?' I try to reassure her, before

changing topic. 'So, I went to see a doctor. I took your advice,' I confide, slightly embarrassed because it feels like I'm taking the attention away from Kofi, but I need to talk to her. I need to talk to *her* and no one else about this. She'll understand that *I* did this, *I* made this choice.

Pryia waits for more, twisting the cap off a bottle of water.

'And after a lot of questions and a lot of talking she's prescribed me some tablets.' There's something wrong enough with me that I need to take something to correct it, to change the natural me. But I'm going to take these tablets. If I want to be able to function in the real world, then this is what I need to do. 'And I told Callie, I told her everything,' I add.

'That must be such a relief, to not have to hide it from her anymore?'

'Sort of. We're not talking right now, well, she won't talk to me anyway, so it's not like we're going to be having big heart to hearts about it,' I tell her.

'You'll work it out,' she says breezily, which annoys me.

'I've tried everything. She won't even open the front door when I call round.'

'Try harder. She's worth it, isn't she? So, you telling your mum next, yes?' she pushes.

'Ha! No chance. Mum's not talking to me either.'

She rolls her eyes as if this is all my fault. Maybe it is.

'So, what tablets are you on?' she asks, switching back to

me. She looks more comfortable talking about periods and PMDD than she does talking about lumbar punctures and Kofi. I guess because she's way ahead of me. She's on familiar ground.

'Flu something,' I tell her, trying to remember the name, 'I've got to go back in a month and have another appointment. She said they might not work for me, that I might have to try a different kind of tablet. She gave me loads of leaflets – the two of you would get on very well – and a list of some books that might help.'

'My doctor asked me what I'd do if my laptop broke. I told her I'd get it repaired. She told me I'm just being repaired. And so are you, Hope. You are repairing yourself and that's the bravest thing you can do,' she says, and it makes me feel like I don't have to justify myself. I think I could tell her all the things I've done, all the unforgivable words I've said, the thoughts I've had and the relationships I've wrecked. I think I could tell her and she wouldn't be frightened of me, wouldn't look at me like I've got **PMDD** written in permanent marker on my forehead. That I'm something bad or battered and bruised.

'Just remember these three words, they're the best bit of advice my doctor gave me about life, "Things get better,"' she tells me and hugs me. 'Things get better!' she repeats.

'Thanks for your help. I don't think I'd have gone without you,' I mumble into her shoulder.

'Yeah, you would, just might have taken a while longer,

but you'd have got there,' she tells me and it makes my
shoulders drop.

I feel like me
Like the me I want to be.

35

'I'm leaving. I will join my choir in the hotel tonight,' Nonno announces, placing an espresso in front of me. He's only just got back from Cardiff. He left straight after the scene the other night.

'No! Is it because of me?' I ask, ready with an appeal to make him stay, an apology, anything to keep it as the three of us and not the two of us. I can't be the one who pushes him away.

I don't want him to leave me.

I want him to be here always.

I carefully move the espresso away from me, that's the last thing I need.

'Of course not, *piccolina*. It is better that I stay with the rest of my choir and after the Opera House in Manchester it will simply be time for me to go home,' he says, and the last word stabs at me because he still has a home, even without Nonna. He still sees his house, their house, as a home. If he goes, this house won't feel like home. It'll just go back to being somewhere I live, somewhere I sleep and eat and wash and go through the motions. I know it and Mum knows it. But neither of us can say it because it is too sad to say out loud.

'But what about the Singing Medicine concert, can't you stay for that?' I try to keep the whine out of my voice but from the look on his face I fail.

'You and your mother need your space, you need to find your way back to one another,' he replies.

'What do you mean?'

'You push her away, she hides her troubles from you, you both dance the quickstep around each other trying not to cause pain, but it isn't working, is it?' He looks tired. I've made him tired. 'And now it is time to talk, because you cannot wander down separate paths anymore. What if you never find the right path back to each other?' he asks. 'She is all you have. You must treasure her.'

I want to deny it but before I can say anything Mum marches into the kitchen. Her hair is back up in a boring business-like bun. She gives me her 'We don't have time to sit and chat over a leisurely breakfast' face and I nod, keen to avoid another argument in front of Nonno.

'Good morning, Gianni.' She plants a kiss on his cheek as she whisks his espresso away and pours it down the sink. I wait for him to argue with her, but he doesn't say anything. She pours him a fresh orange juice. I watch them together, they've known each other for longer than I've been alive. I wonder what he thought of her when Dad first brought her home to Italy. Did he like her? Did he approve?

I sigh. I don't want him to go. This feels like my fault. If I'd been better behaved or less awkward, or just normal, then he wouldn't be talking about hotels.

'It is not your fault, *piccolina*,' he whispers into my ear as I kiss him goodbye, but I shake my head. It is my fault and we both know it.

36

I manage to convince Nonno to stay for a meal before leaving for the hotel, determined to make up for ruining his champagne moment and for swearing at Mum. I offer to cook. I am a flukey cook: sometimes it works and tastes amazing, other times not so much. I don't know which it will be tonight.

'This smells good,' Mum tells me with a hint of surprise as she sits down. She doesn't say my name. She holds that back when she's cross with me and for some reason it hurts. But I don't say anything, I don't make a fuss. Tonight's mission is simple: to show Nonno I can behave, cook a meal like a grown-up and not argue with anyone, not even Mum.

'*Buon appetito!*' Nonno adds as he tastes my chicken. I've gone for a roast, it feels safe.

Dad and I cooked most Sundays while Mum sang in church with the choir. We'd prep vegetables, parboil the potatoes, then roast them with parsnips, honey and oil. He always made his own stuffing which Mum used to say he could have sold in the shops. We haven't had a roast in a very long time.

'Is this Dad's stuffing?' Mum asks as she loads up a forkful. This is her version of a peace offering, or heading in that direction.

'Yep, is it any good?' I want her approval. She nods, her mouth full.

'So are you going to tell us what you're going to put in that extraordinary box, *piccolina*?' Nonno asks before tasting a parsnip. 'Is it a present for Callie?' When he says her name my stomach twists.

'Yeah, but I don't know if there's much point in making it now.'

Mum's face tells me to drop the self-pity act quickly, so I do. I guess she's on Callie's side.

'Some stuff from Guides, I think; posters we made for our gang in Year 8; friendship bands; a few snow globes; and some letters we sent each other when we tried to invent that language…' I stop as the memory makes me cringe.

'Oh, that dreadful gobbledegook you tried to talk to each other in, and you thought Dad and I couldn't understand it!' Mum groans, making Nonno smile. We all think about laughing, but before any of us have really committed to it, there's a noise in the background. It sounds like the timer on the oven, but then I tune in properly and recognise it.

My phone is buzzing. A text. For a moment I hope it's

Callie but there's no way she'd be texting me, not yet – I've got a lot more making up to do first. My phone's next to the sink, directly behind Mum. She picks it up and reaches over to pass it to me but the screen lights up. I haven't locked it. I've been obsessively checking it the whole time I was cooking, texting Callie, sending her funny photos and gifs to no response. Mum glances at the message, then she swipes it open. I sit there speechless for a second, before I find my voice.

'Mum! Are you reading my texts? Give me my phone!'

'Who's Riley?'

Nonno looks from Mum to me and clears his throat. The food sits on our plates, the steam still rising. I want to pick up my plate and throw it at her. I've worked so hard on this meal. I wanted tonight to be about peace. I wanted to show Nonno that he could stay here, that he could cancel his hotel reservation, and now it's all ruined because of my stupid phone, Mum's nosiness and Riley.

'Oh my God! Give me my phone, Mum! *Please*?'

She scrolls through more texts. I jump up; my chair topples over. She holds the phone away, out of reach, and looks at me. She's furious, even more angry than when I swore at her the other night.

'Who the hell is Riley?'

I hear Nonno sigh gently as he pushes his chair back. He leaves the room, but she doesn't even notice. She won't take her eyes off me.

I pick my chair up off the floor and talk myself out of throwing it across the room. I need to try and focus, to find out exactly what she's read.

Then it sinks in – he must have texted me! Riley has texted me! I can't keep the delight off my face.

'Don't you bloody laugh! How dare you? This is not a laughing matter, young lady. Sit down there right now and explain yourself!' She points to the chair.

'I'm not laughing at you, I promise. What do you want me to say?' I ask. Who knows what Riley might have put in a text? The smile comes off pretty quick, the happy feeling in my stomach turns to water. I am desperate to get my hands on my phone and find out what he's just texted.

She throws it at me but I can't catch it in time. It lands with a smash on the floor, echoed by another crash from upstairs.

'Mum!' I shout as she stalks out of the room. I can hear her marching up the stairs, probably going to see what the crash was.

I pick up my phone. There's a crack across the screen but I can just about make out what she must have seen before she threw it on the floor. But it doesn't matter because she's screaming, calling out my name from upstairs.

'Hope! *Hope*? Call an ambulance! Call an ambulance, *now*!'

When I walk onto his ward, he's sitting up in bed in someone else's pyjamas. When I look closer I see they have a stamp on them 'Property of Shrewsbury Hospital'. He'd never wear checks. There are other men in beds. They all look like someone's grandfather. I can't make eye contact with any of them, desperate not to see them all vulnerable and weak. I just keep looking at Nonno. He's smiling but it hurts him, I can see it. I bend over to kiss him, trying hard only to touch his cheek. He's hot and he doesn't smell like Nonno; he smells of hospitals.

'*Piccolina*,' he says and I hear it all in his voice. He's tired of this. He wants to go home. I can't keep him here, not now. I feel toxic. Mum sits on the chair over on the other side of his bed, like I'm contagious.

'Nonno, I'm so sorry,' I start, but he lifts his papery hand, tea-stained and tender. His skin has changed colour already. He's only been in here a day. Is that all it takes to strip yourself away from you, to institutionalise you? He's a patient now, there are notes on him somewhere, a nurse will have taken his temperature and blood. I feel like I should break him out of here, release him back into the sunshine where he belongs. But he looks tired. And so does Mum.

'Now, tell me you've brought me some decent food? *Sì?*' he tries a joke and I fake a smile before passing him the food bag I put together at home.

'What did the doctor say, Gianni?' Mum asks, ignoring me and my food.

'Another day or two of observations and then freedom!' He winks at me.

'But what did she say?' Mum presses.

'Is my heart, but we knew this, *no?*'

The news floors me. It sinks its teeth and talons into my skin, grinding my bones into the cold hospital floor. I've heard of broken hearts, but that felt like a fairy tale. Looking at Nonno, I can see this is real. Is his heart broken, like Dad's, like Nonna's?

'Can't they fix it?' I ask him.

'Yes, I change everything and that will fix it, or slow it down,' he nods reassuringly.

'And you knew?' I ask Mum. I try to keep the tone out of my voice. 'You knew all this time and didn't tell me?' My hand creeps into Nonno's. His nails are too long and his whiskers need attention.

'Yes, but it isn't as bad as you think. Gianni will stop smoking that vile pipe, cut out the espressos and stop eating such a cholesterol-rich diet,' Mum explains. 'It isn't the same as your dad, or Nonna.' But I can't trust her now. She's kept this from me.

'*Why* didn't you tell me?'

'You have had enough to worry about, *piccolina*,' Nonno says. 'I told your *mamma* not to tell you. I wanted to tell you myself but there hasn't been the right time.' Mum nods. And I know why there hasn't been the right time. Because I've taken up all his time.

I say to Mum, 'Half the time you're telling me to grow up and act like an adult and the other half of the time you're treating me like a child who should be kept in the dark?'

She doesn't try to justify it or apologise.

'So what happens now?' I ask.

'We carry on,' Nonno says, as if it's simple. Who knows, maybe it is. 'We beat on, boats against the current, borne back ceaselessly into the past.'

'What?' I am lost but Mum's smiling, as if this makes sense to her.

Everyone in my family has a broken heart and I don't know how to fix any of them.

Nonno's asleep but I can't leave. The nurse has finally left us on our own, after giving me a mini-lecture on cholesterol and heart disease and yet another stupid leaflet. I want to ban hospitals leaflets. I want to gather them all up in a heap and set them on fire. I want to go home, get his clothes and give the hospital theirs back. I want to clip his whiskers, brush his hair and make him look like Nonno again.

When Mum goes to get a coffee, I check he's still breathing. I sneak my hand underneath his nose – the hairs on the back of my hand tickle. He's fine, for now.

I get my phone out and read Riley's text again. What a stupid thing to send, no wonder Mum freaked out. It sounds so dodgy, so *him*.

Let's do it.
I want to do it with you!
Name the time and place.

As if nothing has happened. As if he hasn't been MIA for weeks now. I haven't got anything to do while I sit here and wait for Mum to come back, so I text back.

Fuck off
She's alive! The one with the foul mouth.
Fuck right off!
Ah, now don't be angry. There's been heavy family shite going on here. I would have texted you sooner.
Tell someone who gives a shit.
Fair play, I'm a gobshite but a very sorry one. I did try

and phone you, remember? Now, do you still want to meet up?

Tell me about this heavy family stuff that meant you were unable to text me for weeks.

It wasn't weeks now, was it? In case no one's mentioned this before you can be a real drama queen.

Start talking.

My sister left to go to uni without saying goodbye to my da. He didn't even want her to go. She took the coward's way out and left Da a note, on the kitchen table of all places. The state of her! Da turned into a lunatic & made me farm manager. Good craic had by all!

And…

And that's why I've been ignoring you, alright? I was embarrassed. Going on about all me travels and 80 days round the world and all that. Never going to happen now.

Sounds like a right mess.

Yeah. And I'm shamed. You must think I'm a right loser. I want to be a million miles from here but I'm stuck. I'm starting to hate him.

We all hate our parents at some point.

C'mon now there's you go-getting and doing all the shite you said you would and I'm knee deep in cow shit. Back to arses, hey? Nothing changes.

I'm not doing anything other than making a mess of everything.

What do you mean?

Long story. I can't see my screen properly cos it's a bit smashed (part of the long story mess) so I'm going to phone you. Alright?

Are you sure? Like, now?

Yeah, why not? Let's act like normal human beings. I'm done with hiding all the time.

Fair play to you. I should warn you I'm hardly a riot at the moment. Serious now, I might have even run out of jokes.

I'm in hospital, not working, not a riot either.

Shite, are you alright? What's happened?

I'm ringing, you better answer.

And before I can chicken out I dial his number and he actually answers. I tell him all about what happened with Nonno. And Mum. And Callie. It feels like I recognise his voice, as if we've been talking all this time instead of texting. He sounds familiar when he tells me about all the arguments between his sister and his dad. And once he's started he can't stop talking: how trapped he is, how stuck. And I can't stop asking him questions about what his sister said and where she's gone and why. Just when I think *alright, that's enough, no more for tonight* and I go to end the call, I can't because he needs me. *He* needs me this time. And for some reason that feels good.

38

'You're here!' Pryia shouts, when I walk into the staffroom on Monday morning.

'Err, yeah. No need for the cheerleading squad, Pryia!' I joke, not really expecting such enthusiasm this early in the morning. I finish my text to Callie and put my phone away. I shamelessly had to namedrop Nonno and tell her what happened, but it worked, she rang me straightaway and then turned up at the hospital. Mum and I haven't been into work for a few days, because of Nonno. Between Mum and me and Callie's visits, he's been kept busy.

'Kofi's asking for you,' she says. She's still pretty loud.

'I'll be there in a minute, let me just...' I turn to pick up a purple bucket of instruments. Pryia grabs my shoulders and spins me round. I drop the bucket.

'There's no time. You've got to come now.' I see the panic in her eyes.

'Why?' I ask but I don't need to. I hear it in her voice.

'He was taken into ICU over the weekend,' she replies, and simply takes my hand and holds it in hers. 'Hope? Are you okay?' Pryia asks. She sounds like an echo, as if she's said my name a few times but I'm only just hearing it.

'Let's go.' I let her lead me past Kofi's room, up the stairs towards ICU. I force myself to read the sign. It's black and white. Not yellow. *This isn't Dad. This is someone else.* I stand outside the door. I push it open and the door handle clashes with the wall. I walk into the room. I keep talking to myself in my head: *I can do this.*

'Kofi!' I say it loudly, so I can't hear the beeping. My voice doesn't sound like me but at least there's sound. He's in what looks like a cot. It's a bed but with rails. He is lying very flat on his back. I can only really see his face. He has tubes coming out of his nose and something over his mouth that must be oxygen. His mum sits on a chair next to his bed. She looks smaller, shrunken. There are nurses everywhere but it's really quiet. Everyone's whispering and walking softly, trying hard not to make any noise. His eyes are closed but his chest is moving up and down. I watch it for several seconds until Pryia's words filter through.

'Mrs Agard has asked us to come and sing to Kofi,' she explains unnecessarily to the nurses. They nod. Kofi's mum doesn't even look up at us, her eyes are on Kofi the whole time.

I start singing, keeping my eyes on the rise and fall of

230

Kofi's chest. And Kofi breathes on and on with the help of a ventilator which

Clicks and whirs
Clicks and whirs
Clicks and whirs.

Mum's waiting for me in the staffroom at the end of the day. I cry without holding back. I don't really notice who else is in there. She wraps her arms around me until I'm able to talk.

'He looks too small in the bed,' I say into her shoulder. She doesn't reply. 'And his mum has shrunk, she's lost so much weight. All I can do is stand there and sing stupid songs.' I pull back to look at her.

'They aren't stupid. They mean something to you and Kofi. You've built up a bond. Believe it or not, you're helping him and his mum,' she tries to reassure me. 'That's all you can do right now.' She's right, but somehow it doesn't feel enough. Today it doesn't feel anywhere near enough.

'Here.' She hands me my mobile, which I thought I'd left in my locker, but I'm too shocked to take it. It falls to the floor.

'Don't smash the screen! I've only just got it repaired. Had to sneak it out of your locker at lunchtime,' she tells me, trying to smile.

'Why?'

'Because if I can't trust you, who can I trust? You didn't feel you could tell me about this Riley boy, you couldn't confide in me, and that means something has gone wrong. I should have told you about Nonno's heart problems and his crazy cholesterol levels. You're right, I should have talked to you. You're not a baby anymore,' she admits.

'Even if I act like one?'

'Even then,' she says, brushing my hair out of my face.

'If we're doing the whole full-disclosure thing, there's something I'd better tell you.'

'Worse than that you've got a secret Irish boyfriend who you've been sneakily messaging?' She tries to say it lightly, but it sounds loaded. I can hear how much its cost her to try and make a joke out of the secrets I've been keeping, which makes what I'm about to tell her even worse.

'Yes. There's something worse than having a secret boyfriend, not that he's my boyfriend but...' I'm getting confused. 'I'd better tell you that we've been on the phone talking for most of the weekend.' She doesn't say anything so I carry on. 'But I didn't just bump into him on the ferry, Mum, that's not how it happened, I...'

Mum stands up and holds out her hand to me. 'Let's get out of here.'

We walk out into the garden of remembrance, which is unusually quiet. She sits down on a bench and pats it. She's trying so hard. She thinks this is going to be a mother-daughter chat and whatever I've got to tell her can't be that bad. But it is. It really is.

'He saved me,' I tell her.

She frowns but stops herself from saying anything.

'I was… I was in a panic, a real state. I'd failed and I didn't want to go home and I didn't know what to do. Everyone else was in the restaurant celebrating and I went for a walk on the deck in the rain. I wasn't with them anymore. I didn't have anyone to talk to and it was the worst time it could have happened, everything's always worse when…'

This time she stops me because I am not making sense to her.

'What's always worse?' she asks, confused.

'Because it was the week before,' I tell her, hoping she'll get it.

'Week before what? A date? An anniversary?' I can tell she is searching her mind for dates about Dad.

'No. It was *never* about Dad,' I tell her and she moves away from me a little. I'm shouting. I try to lower my voice.

'The week before is always the worst. The week before my period.'

She looks visibly relieved. She is thinking, 'Oh, that again. Hope and her mood swings, hormonal, always been a bit overly sensitive.' And I want to stand on the bench and rip my clothes off and show her the worst of me, what's inside me right now crawling to get out. I want her to see *me* in the garden of remembrance amongst all the pretty flowers. All the ugly things I hide from her – all the weeds that wind their way through me, squeezing the life out of everything. But the tablets must be starting to work, I can feel the weeds but they can't pull me under today. I carry on and tell her what I need to tell her, what I *should* have told her before.

'I've got PMDD. I'm on tablets. Premenstrual Dysphoric Disorder. I have to say it slowly because sometimes I get the D bits mixed up. These tablets, I think they're working. I think I'm going to be alright,' I tell her. I feel like the parent. She looks terrified. Acronyms are dangerous, they're much scarier than real words. 'Premenstrual Dysphoric Disorder,' I repeat, wondering if the words sound any better than the acronym.

'What the bloody hell is that?' I can see all the terrifying words racing through her mind. Cancer? Life threatening? Dying? Tablets? Hospital? Surgery? Gynaecologist?

'It's sort of like PMT but much worse, so much worse, but that's the quick and easy way to explain it.' And as soon as I've said PMT, the panic visibly shrinks from her eyes, and she looks relieved again. But it isn't as straightforward as I've made it sound.

'I get angry, violent, aggressive, irrational and can't see or hear or realise what I'm doing or saying. Sometimes I don't even remember what I've said. I don't even see it the next day or the day after sometimes. I only see it when my period turns up – it's like something bursts or clears and I see it all then – especially if there's damage, like in my room, or words I've said. The words come back to me, late at night, when I'm trying to sleep. Then it all comes back to punch me in the face.' I try to put it into my own words, rather than the formal language on the leaflet. 'I can't concentrate on what people are saying, sometimes I don't even hear them,' I tell her.

But it isn't enough. There's more.

'I was on the ferry. It was chucking it down and I needed to get away from their laughing and celebrating and being disgustingly happy in their success. I hated them, even Callie. I *know*, Mum, I *know*, so don't look at me like that. You know how I feel about Callie, that's why I was so scared. If I felt like that about *her*, I knew there was something really wrong with me. Please, just let me get this out?' I have to keep going. 'I didn't want to come home and face you, not that this is your fault, it *really* isn't. I knew what we'd agreed to and once I told you that would be it – The End. So I went for a walk on the deck and it was raining and raining and it was making me even angrier. My hair wouldn't stay out of my eyes and I was crying too and I climbed up onto the safety rail. I was screaming and shouting and crying and swearing and then I wobbled and someone – Riley – grabbed me and pulled me down. He isn't a hero, actually he's a bit of an arse, but he did save me. That's who he is and that's how we met.' I look up at her. 'That's the truth. All of it, this time.'

'But you weren't actually going to do something stupid, were you? Were you really going to do *that*?' She can't bring herself to say suicide.

'No.' I tell her the truth. 'I was raging but I wasn't suicidal, I promise. But it's just I can't be sure of anything in that week: what I'm doing, where I'm going, if I'm safe or not. It's a bit like being *Alice in Wonderland*, everything looks the same but it's all changed, including me,' I try to explain.

'You don't ever have to feel like that again. Nothing is too big or too awful that we can't deal with it, together. I know you think that you've run out of choices, but you haven't. You're right at the start of everything and part of the adventure is not knowing what's going to happen.' She crushes me with her body, as if she can pour all her love into me. 'And whatever happens, Hope, I will be there with you, every single step of the way.' She kisses me hard on my cheek. 'You are strong, smart and more than capable. I *know* it.'

I feel her heartbeat and I let go of something. I don't know what exactly, but something leaves me. We sit and breathe in the strongly scented air as all the birds start singing.

September

Nonno is out of hospital in time for my first choir rehearsal on Monday night. He sits down slowly on the back pew, takes his hat off, smoothes his hair and then places the hat on the seat next to him. Mum forced him to wear a coat, despite his protests, but a British summer is not quite the same as an Italian one. He gave in and was wrapped up and was probably sweating before we even left the house. I join Mum and the others for the warm-up.

When Nonno holds up one hand, it means I can hear you, you're hitting that back wall. His seal of approval means more to me than I had thought it could. I can't take my eyes off him as I sing, like I have to keep checking him. I'm so glad that he didn't go home: the doctor wouldn't let him fly back yet. I get him for a bit longer and this time I'm not going to ruin it.

I raise my voice and feel it settling down around me like a blanket. Mum sneaks her hand into mine, out of sight of the others, and gives it a tiny squeeze and for a moment I forget everything else and just let the music hold me. Nonno starts singing at the back of the church. I can see his lips moving and, even though I can't hear him, I know he's with me.

When we get back from choir Nonno offers to walk Scout and Mum seizes the moment. I think Mum's decided it's up to me to tell him but I can only just cope with her reaction for now. All these secrets – I thought we were such a straightforward family. I guess there's no such thing.

'I've been researching what you told me and talked to a few people at work and I'd like you to see someone. We can see her together if you like, or you can go on your own, whatever you want. She's called Dr Dee and...' Mum stops when she sees my smile.

'My GP recommended her. That's who I'm on a waiting list to see.'

'Oh, right, well I guess the field isn't that big for PMDD. I mean, I'd never heard of it before, I'm ashamed to say.' Mum carries on, tucking my hair behind my ear. I can sense she wants to reach out and hold me. 'There's online groups you can join and support groups and I know I can't fully understand what you're going through, but I can listen. If it doesn't freak you out too much we can synch our cycles,' she suggests, which makes me burst out laughing.

'How?'

'I thought you'd already know, Ms Smarty Pants. Through our Clue accounts. Then I'll know … you know, where you are in the month and that kind of thing.'

'You've joined too?'

'Should have done it ages ago.' She throws it off as nothing but once again she's surprised me.

'Thanks, Mum.' I kiss her on her cheek and she grabs the opportunity and holds me tight.

'I can't believe you've been going through this by yourself, making appointments to see doctors and getting help. I wish I'd known. I wish you'd felt you could tell me.' She sounds hurt. 'I thought it was something else, I thought it was,' she pauses before she says his name, 'about Dad.'

I shake my head. 'I wish people would stop thinking everything is about Dad. I mean, I know it should be but sometimes it isn't.'

She nods her head, like she gets it. 'You're so brave.' I can hear the pride in her voice.

I think about all the kids on Pan Ward. That's what I see when I hear the word brave – bandages and blood – but maybe you don't need to *see* brave to know it's there? Maybe brave isn't what I thought it was.

'What happened? What's gone wrong?'

'Complications,' Pryia says.

'I thought Kofi was in recovery, I thought he was getting better?'

'He developed multiple complications. His mum told me he went into septic shock and respiratory distress while we were all at choir last night,' she croaks, her voice breaking a little. She's trying not to cry. I don't know what septic means.

We stand in the corridor in silence, watching people going about their business as if it's any old Tuesday morning. Nurses, doctors, consultants, cleaners, patients, parents, all walking, talking, coming, going, and we just linger there, leaning against the wall as if it can hold us up.

'They've done everything they can. It was working, but his body hasn't reacted how they thought it would. His burns are…' she runs out of words.

I can't believe there's nothing they can do. He's eleven. *Eleven.*

'They put him on the ECMO machine, like an artificial lung, but it didn't work. His heart failed and then his other... his other organs failed too. He's on the ventilator but...' She can't carry on. 'His mum's asked if we'll sing to him...'

I get ready to say yes, of course, but she shakes her head.

'*Wait*, Hope. Just wait a minute. You can't just say yes, alright, a lot of people can't handle this.' She pauses. 'Come on, let's talk outside.'

I follow her down the stairs into the garden. Why do people keep going to the garden to talk? You can't exactly escape from the hospital by stepping outside, it's still there.

She sits down on a bench and waits for me to join her. I'm starting to hate this bench.

'It's called an end-of-life event. Some parents ask us to sing to their children when they've ... when they come to the end.' She struggles to get the words out.

All I hear is END. THE END in capital letters. My heart changes rhythm. My heart relocates to my throat. There's a rapid *boom, boom, boom* as if I've be given a shot of adrenalin. Dad and Nonna's faces flicker in front of me.

THE END.

'How can he be at his end?' I ask in disbelief. She doesn't have the answers.

We are quiet for a while, before going back. 'I can do this,' I say with confidence I don't really feel.

'Don't say yes to something that you might not be able to cope with, please.'

What does she want us to sing to him?' I ask, as we walk back up to ICU.

'Shouldn't you check with your mum first? She might say no.' Pryia hovers on the stairs.

'She'll say yes.' I know Mum will understand and want me do this. Pryia follows me reluctantly.

I think back to Fatima and the organ-donor conversation, how she warned me time wasn't on her side. There's no time now. I open the door to Kofi's room. Mum's already in there with Nikhil, Owen is sitting next to Kofi's mum, holding her hand. They're waiting for us.

We form a semi-circle by the bed. The nurses seem to retreat, melting away into the background. The room is quiet, apart from the sound of the ventilator huffing as we start to sing. I look at Kofi's face, his skin, his black lashes resting on his cheeks, his hair gently starting to curl over his ears and his chest moving up and down. I scan him for signs that he can hear us. I move closer to him. I wish it were just him and me.

But now I'm here
I'm in the room
And I will sing
goodbye
This time.

I can see his lips beneath the oxygen mask. I reach out and touch the soft skin on his face, the only part of him not red or white, not burned or damaged. I join in with the chorus, determined to sing the notes long and loud as we say goodbye.

Callie eventually opens the door. I fall into her hallway. I'm crying but I've gone past the point where I care. She doesn't wrap her arms around me. She doesn't ask me what's wrong. She just slumps down onto the floor next to me, leaving the front door wide open. I wonder if Mum's phoned her, to warn her. I try to breathe properly but I'm still gulping. I've been keeping it in all the way over on the bus and I can't any longer.

'He's dead,' I tell her. She looks panicked, then bursts into tears too.

'When? *When*?'

The house sounds empty. I wonder where her family are.

'This afternoon. We had to sing to him. I sang to him.'

'What? Why did you sing to him?' She looks confused.

'Because that's what his mum wanted.' I feel sick, shaky and drained.

'Whose mum? What are you going on about?' Callie's got her hand on my arm now.

'Kofi.'

She snatches her arm away. '*Shit*! I thought you meant Nonno! I thought Nonno had died. *Oh my God*!' She looks relieved.

'I never said Nonno. He's doing much better.'

'You should have said. You should have said it was that kid.' She points at me, like I've got something wrong again.

'He's not just some kid. He's *Kofi*.' I wipe my face and sit up, my back against their radiator. She does the same. We look at each other.

'What happened?' she asks eventually.

'Complications, septic shock.' I still don't really know what it means.

'And you sang to him? As he died?' She looks horrified. 'You sat there and sang?'

'Yes, I guess. I mean, I think the machine was doing all the breathing and stuff for him. But yeah, we sang to him.'

'Could he hear you? I mean, was there any point?'

'I hope he could hear us. Even if he couldn't, his mum could and I know it helped her,' I answer.

'I just can't believe you did that. You sat there and sang to him with other people in the room? *How*? How did you not just break down or run out of the room? I don't know you at all. I thought I knew *everything* about you.'

For a moment I think she means it like she did before,

in my room, but it sounds different, it sounds like understanding. 'You keep on surprising me,' she says, shuffling a little closer to me.

'I'm sorry,' I say, carefully putting my arm around her. 'I'll try to stop.'

'No, don't,' she says after a bit.

'Alright then.'

'Alright then.' And we sit there like that, on her hallway floor, half crying, half not, talking about everything, with the front door wide open, as the late summer evening creeps in around us.

43

You haven't answered me all day.

…

Hope? Are you ok? Haven't heard from you. Has something happened?

I've had the worst day of my life. Can't think of any words big enough to cover it.

What's happened now? I can't keep up with you and your capers.

A boy died today.

Ah, sorry. I'm sorry for your troubles. Was it the boy on the burns unit?

How did you know?

I know he's important to you. He sounded like a grand kid. What happened?

Complications. He had a cardiac arrest. His heart just gave up. Same as Nonna and just like my dad.

Your dad? Can I call you?

No. It's too late.

Tell me something about your dad then, something that won't upset you.

He's a music teacher. Well, was head of music. He was doing a concert in Birmingham with his choir. It was a big competition thing called Young Voices and he had a heart attack during the afternoon rehearsal. They got him to the hospital but it wasn't any good. He had another one in the ambulance. He was on a ventilator when I got there. Sorry, I'm supposed to be telling you nice stuff about him. Sorry to go on about my dad.

Don't be. What was his name? What did he look like?

Frank to his friends, Franco to my grandparents and of course Dad to me. When I was little he tried to get me to call him Papà but apparently I wasn't having any of it, none of my friends called their fathers Papà and I guess I wanted to be like everyone else. He was tall and had a big nose and massive hands and he was always singing. I remember him reading Roald Dahl stories to me at night and thinking that he looked a bit like the BFG but without the huge ears. He always wore bright colours, never black, and he hated strawberries.

Fair enough.

That's a bit random isn't it but you did ask. I'm going to stop now.

Hope? Are you still there?

Yep.

Do you want to talk about the boy?

No. Yes. He had this thing about *Doctor Who*, completely obsessed with it. He wanted to work on set and now… It just sucks, life sucks.

Not always but yeah, it does sometimes.

I had to sing to him, sing him to sleep.

I don't know what to say to that. I don't think I could do it. You're so brave.

God! Has someone hacked your account, Riley? I'm not brave. I'm a right mess.

Well, a lot of people would disagree.

I know we said no jokes but I think this one might help. Could we lift the ban for one night? I promise it's not really a man walked into a bar kind of joke, it's better than that. Can I tell you the one about the man in a flood? Can I call you? It's a wee bit long.

No, I don't want to talk.

We won't talk, I promise. I'll just tell you the joke and then I'll put the phone down.

Promise?

Swear.

Before I can change my mind my phone rings. I swipe to answer straightaway.

'Hello? Hope?'

'This joke better have a decent punchline.'

'Alright… A man is caught in a flood. He climbs onto the roof of his house and trusts that God will rescue him.

A neighbour floats past in a canoe and says, "Get in."

"'No thanks," says the man. "I've just said a prayer to God. He will save me."

'Later the police come by in a boat. "Get in. We'll rescue you."

"'No thanks," says the man. "I've just said another prayer to God, I'm sure he will save me."

'Then a helicopter hovers over him and lets down a rope ladder. "Climb this ladder and we'll fly you to safety," they shout.

"'No thanks," says the man. "I've prayed to God, I know he will save me."

'All this time the water has continued to rise, until soon it reaches above the roof of the man's house and he is drowned. When he gets to heaven he finds God and asks him, "Why am I here? I prayed to you. I asked you to save me. I trusted you to save me from that flood."

"'Yes you did, my child," replied the Lord. "And I sent you a canoe, a boat and a helicopter, but you didn't get in. You wouldn't let those people help you. That is why you are in heaven."

'Night then, Hope.'

'Night, Riley.'

44

'Hope, are you going to put that thing down? Is that him again? Are you sure I shouldn't call his parents, just to introduce myself?' Mum asks, looking over her shoulder at the oncoming traffic.

'No! Just, *no*! You promised?'

She takes her hands off the wheel and holds them up in defeat. I'm still not used to her knowing about Riley.

'Hope? Was there something you wanted to talk about?' Mum taps me on the arm. I wonder when she painted her nails, she hasn't done them in ages.

'Sorry, right. Um…' I've completely forgotten what I wanted to talk to her about. My mind is totally empty.

And then I remember him. My brain places a photograph in my head and I hear the last chorus and see Kofi's face and I know I'll dream about him again tonight.

'I need to stop coming into work with you. I'm sorry but I just can't do this anymore,' I confess, instantly feeling a failure.

'You want to audition again?' she asks, and she's making her voice flat and calm, pretending that this is fine with her.

I picture the small white box in my top drawer at home with my name and address printed on it. I think of the colours of my medicine, the green and yellow capsules, and I close my eyes for a second and breathe out in relief. I'm not going to do or say anything I shouldn't, anything I'll want to die over when I play it back in my head like evidence. I'm not going to do that.

'Um, no, I don't actually,' I reply. And I mean it.

'*Really*?'

'Yes, really.'

'What's changed?' She wants to know. She looks relieved.

'Everything.'

She's checking her mirrors as she pulls out into the middle lane to get around a lorry, but I can see she's happy although she's trying to keep a lid on it, in case I change my mind.

'I've been talking to Callie after... after we sang, you know... I told Callie about this course that's just started running in Birmingham. I knew about it ages ago. I saw a poster up in the staffroom about it but I don't think I was ready to think about it then. When I got brave enough to phone them it was too late, I'd missed the deadline.' I try and fill her in as quickly as possible.

'Stop. What course?'

'I spoke to admissions yesterday. I rang them up and told them I wanted to put my name down for next year and, well, it turns out someone's dropped out, before it's even started!' I'm talking too fast.

'What's the course, Hope?' Mum asks again. I'm trying her patience.

'It's Birmingham Music School – part of Birmingham Theatre School, the one Callie's going to, but it's not acting, I mean, they do acting, but that's not why I'm going.'

'Are you sure?'

'I'm sure, Mum. When I went to the RSC, I watched them all talking about their characters, analysing the meaning behind their lines, trying out different voices and accents and I loved every single second of it. If they'd offered me an apprenticeship or even a job as their tea girl, I'd have taken it. But now...' I take a big breath, before launching into my sales pitch. 'After Kofi and what happened with Nonno, everything's changed. *I've* changed. I don't know what I'm changing into, which scares me, but I want to find out. And maybe *if* I get in, I will.'

I am desperate for her to understand, to get *me*, even though I can't properly explain myself.

'Hope, what is the course?' she says so slowly. I realise I still haven't answered her.

'Oh God! Sorry, *sorry*! Music, BTEC Level 3 diploma in music and songwriting.'

'Songwriting? Ah, I see, well, that makes sense.'

'I can do this, Mum. I think I'll be good at it.' I really mean it.

'I think so too. I'm so glad you're writing again,' she says, completely surprising me. 'Do you think Singing Medicine might be something you can come back to? I'm going to need new team members if we carry on expanding the way we are. Something to think about, after you've done your music course? Or you could even teach music, if you wanted to, like your dad?'

'Maybe,' I say and I mean it.

'What happens next?'

'I've got an audition, a singing audition,' I clarify, 'and *if* I pass it then I'm in and I can start with everyone else at the end of the month. *If* I pass that is.' I finish, then close my mouth before I say anymore or jinx the whole thing.

'You'll get in, love.'

'Maybe,'

'*Definitely*. I think you might have found your plan B.'

45

Because I was rehearsing. There's a big concert coming up, you might remember me mentioning it eleventy billion times over the last few weeks? I've never sung with the choir in public before. This'll be my first gig with them. In front of other people, real live human people.

Eleventy billion? You did mention maths wasn't your strong point. Right, I just thought you were ignoring me.

Ugh, you're so needy! Haven't you got anything else to do other than message me?

Yeah, yeah. I'm actually going to be very busy soon but right now I'm bored.

So, I'm just a handy time filler?

Yep. So are you nervous?

What about?

She's so casual! Performing at the concert, the one you can't stop mentioning. And there's the matter of that BIG audition you've got coming up. Don't think I didn't notice you avoiding the topic.

Shut up. You're the one who avoids topics.

Harsh Hope they should call you.

But true. Have you even booked any tickets yet?

How can I? I'm working full-time until Da finds a new manager. I'll book something then.

Ready for some Harsh Hope? I think if you don't book something now you never will and you'll just stay on the farm. FOREVER. Is that what you're scared of?

Way harsh, Hope.

I'm serious, you need to book those tickets, then tell your dad and escape while you still can before you start talking to the cows like they're your friends.

Too late for that. Daisy's got some great hair tips she shared with me this morning.

I'm being serious. You need to do this. Make a commitment, spend some money and then you can't chicken out. One life, just do it!

Wrong slogan. So what are you singing in this concert then?

Nothing you'd have heard of. And stop dodging my questions.

Savage!

Soz ☺

Smiley face? Soz? Now I know you're nervous!

Actually singing calms me down. I feel good when I sing. Anyway, the concert will be fun. You should come.

257

I send it before I can stop my fingers. The last time I invited Riley to meet me he disappeared. Why did I do that? I'm texting without thinking, chucking invites around as if last time never happened.

Thought you'd never ask.

What does that mean?

Didn't feel I could invite myself but I've been hoping (ha! See what I did there) that you'd ask me.

...

So can I come? Is it alright?

Maybe, I mean, sure. On one condition.

Ah man, I knew it. There's always strings attached with you isn't there. Sure, you only want me for my body!

Shut up. You have to book a ticket to somewhere, anywhere. And you HAVE to tell your dad. DEAL?

You drive a hard bargain Ms Caps Lock.

Is that a yes, Dublin?

Yes!

Good, now go away I've got something important to do.

I switch from texting Riley to texting Callie.

Cal, you ready to do this?

Ready and on my way.

I turn on my computer and open the organ donor page, knowing that Callie is doing the same thing at the same time right next to me on her laptop. We've made a pact and it feels less weird than I thought it would. I wasn't sure if she'd say yes. It's a pretty random and weird thing to ask someone to do with you. I click on the website that I've looked at way too many times since I met Fatima. I read the screen again even though I know word for word what it says, but this time is different because Callie is reading it with me, right next to me.

Register your details

Add your name to the NHS Organ Donor Register and one day you may be able to save lives.

All you need to do is fill out this form with your information and preferences and we will do the rest. This form will take no more than **2 minutes** to complete.

I put all my details in – no problem until I get to the bit that asks:

Do you want to donate all organs and tissue?

I have two choices – all or some. I wonder which button Callie will hit. I try not to peek at her screen. Will my heart be any good to anyone? I think about Nonna, Dad and Nonno. No point in half measures, as Fatima said, 'Once you're dead you're dead'. What good are some of my organs to me then? I do want to help someone, loads of people, because I've seen what happens when you run out of options, out of time. I don't want that to happen to anyone else ever again, not if I can help it.

I hit *all*.

I fill out the rest of the form, everything seems easy after that big question, and I submit it. Done.

'You finished?' she asks.

'Yes. You?'

She turns the screen of her laptop so I can see.

'Did you go all in? Give them every last bit of you, even your dodgy eyeballs?' she grins.

'Yuck, but yes. Hopefully my limited eyesight might be of use to someone.'

'Highly hopeful. So that's another thing ticked off your list. Next: your audition. Are you ready? I can just picture our future, you'll be at the Music School and I'll be over the road at the Theatre School and we can wave to each other through the windows,' Callie smiles, 'and blow kisses and meet for coffee…'

'*IF* I get in!' I interrupt. 'We'll be too busy for coffee, you know, like working and studying?'

'Oh yeah, there'll be a bit of that going on, too. As if they wouldn't take you. *Silly.*'

'Aren't we supposed to be putting a plan into action?' I remind her.

'Sorry, I forgot all about *Riley*,' Callie slips into a broad Deep-South American accent.

'Err, he's Irish not American. How did you even get in to drama college?'

I stop. We both look at each other.

'Oh my! Defining moment: Hope makes a joke about drama college. Hope does not break down and cry. Date and time noted.' Callie pretends to make notes in a journal.

'I know, right?' I say, pleased. She nods. 'This is progress. Anyway, back to your awful accent...' I wait for her to switch to Irish.

'Sorry to be sure, *Riley*,' Her Dublin accent is perfect. This – this is what makes *us*. Sitting on the floor in my room talking absolute rubbish with each other. I can't articulate or explain it, but it is there right in front of me – I can almost touch it.

'Right, Plan *Mamma* Erin – first up, make it sound like it's her idea and you'd never really thought of asking Riley to the concert, but now that she mentions it, "Hey, what a great idea." She's been desperate to meet him ever since she found out about him. And of course I can take it or leave it, but seeing as I'm coming to the concert it makes sense for me to meet him too,' Callie says in her super-casual voice.

'Maybe...' I hesitate.

'Definitely. Try and get her to ask someone else to come, like one of her mates or that Gethin or Gavin bloke from book club,' she sniggers.

'More matchmaking? What is with you, trying to pair people up?' I ask. 'I thought you didn't believe in romance?'

261

'I'm just the messenger, but I've seen the covert looks he gives her in The Bird's Nest over their cappuccinos at book club,' Callie says with great authority.

'Good plan, apart from the Gavin fairy tale. She's so not into him.'

Callie shrugs at me as I reach into my wardrobe.

'What you doing?'

'I've got something for you.' I hand her the parcel, wrapped in layers of tissue paper.

'Is that my Hope Chest?' she asks. I nod. 'It's beautiful,' she says, pulling back the wrapping and stroking the wood.

I open the lid and search past the friendship bracelets, the bits of our Guides rug, cut-out blazer badges and all the other things I've put in there to show her what we are to one another. I find it near the bottom. Carefully I take out the snow globe she gave me, the very first one. She peels off the sheet music I've rolled the globe in, opens it up and skim reads it.

'Is this song for me? Is this my song?' she asks then reads the title out loud, '*The Song of Us.*'

I nod, then shake the globe and we both laugh.

'You've never written me a song before. I'll keep this forever, even when I'm really old and can't even remember what you look like or who you are anymore.'

'What about when you can't remember who you are?' I laugh.

'Even then,' she promises. I close the lid of the Hope

Chest. 'Sing it for me?' she asks, and so I do to the tune of her favourite Bangles song, 'I'll Set you Free'. We sit next to one another, holding hands, and I sing as the last flakes of snow fall.

The Song of Us

I remember when we were five
all knowing, so small and wise
The world was free and easy
no reason to hide

And now years later
you still live inside my heart
Even though we both know it,
someday we'll have to part

Chorus

All the things that I can't say
Are reflected back in your eyes
You see past my fake smiles
there's more to me than my lies
More to me than lies

When you are not with me
There's no Us in the world
You're all the things that I can't yet be
Smiles and so confident girl

hopes, wishes and teenage dreams
I'll never stop believing
but nothing's as easy as it seems

Chorus
All the things that I can't say
Are reflected back in your eyes
You see past my fake smiles
there's more to me than my lies

A Life without Us in it
To me is just not a choice
You shout clear and loud
And singing gives me my voice
gives me my voice

So now we'll carry on
What more can we do?
For we are brave and strong
Together somehow, we will make it through

46

I head down into the kitchen to find Mum to put Plan Erin into place but she's got her head on the table.

'Mum, are you okay?' She's clearly far from okay. Why do I keep doing that?

She replies, 'Sffmmnhhm.' I put my arm around her and wait for proper words. 'Nonno's…' she starts, but then hiccups and coughs as the same time.

'Nonno's what?' I scream. *Oh God, where is he? What's happened to him?*

She looks up at me, make-up smudged and hair all over the place. 'No! No, he's fine. Not that, sorry, he's fine. He's still in Manchester – safe and sound. Don't panic. He's staying in the hotel with the rest of his choir tonight, they're off out for a meal somewhere,' she reassures me quickly. 'He's promised me faithfully he'll order low-cholesterol food, no pudding and definitely no grappa.'

'So why are you crying?' I ask, relief making me fall into a chair.

'He's bought us a Christmas present.'

I'm clueless why this has made her cry.

'Of all the rude things! I mean, who does he think he is? Shopping for Christmas presents in September? Disgusting!' I stop joking when she doesn't smile. 'Oh God, it's not another cookbook is it. Don't take it personally. We could open a cookbook library.'

'He wants us to come to Italy. For Christmas! That's so soon, so soon.'

Now I get it. I pull her in tight, just like she would do with me.

'Mum, we can do this. You and me. We can do it,' I tell her over and over, trying to let her know without saying the words that we aren't running away from Christmas without him, that going to Italy isn't a failure. It's the start of us two rather than us three. But I can't say this, they're just thoughts in my head.

'It just took me by surprise. It's already September. Look, he's even bought our tickets so I can't find an excuse. I know I don't want to be here for Christmas, but I'm not sure I want to be over there either. There's memories everywhere. Maybe we should talk about moving again…' She's thinking aloud, not really aware of me for a second, and finally we get to the heart of it.

She cups my face in her hands, which smell of onions. I

manage not to pull away. She's been making spaghetti bolognaise for tea. The tomato sauce is burning on the hob. I don't care about tea or the sauce or the fact that my cheeks will reek of onions all night.

'Things get better,' I tell her.

'When did you get so sensible?'

I wonder what the answer is.

I get up and turn the heat down on the sauce for something to do, while I wonder how shameful it would be to take a tiny little bit of advantage of Mum right now and ask her a question.

'Talking of Nonno, he's coming to our concert, isn't he? Manchester was their last date?' She nods and I charge on before I can change my mind. 'Good. So, is there anyone else you want to invite? I mean, I know people from work are coming and Callie's parents have bought tickets. Any other friends you want to ask?'

She says something about someone in her book group buying a few tickets and looks uncomfortable for a second. Maybe Callie is right about this Gavin one. She's right about most things.

I take my chance, it's now or never.

'I was wondering if this might be a good time for you to meet Riley. I mean, before we go to Italy with Nonno...' I feel guilty for taking advantage of her but keep quiet all the same.

She reaches down into the cupboard to get a pan for the

water. She carries it over to the sink, fills it and puts it on the hob. She gets a packet of spaghetti – Nonno would be horrified. I hope he's found a decent restaurant in Manchester, low-cholesterol food sounds deeply dull. She turns the gas on and waits for the water to heat. She says nothing the whole time the water comes slowly to the boil. I wonder if I've picked the wrong moment. But as the water starts to bubble up she says one word without looking at me.

'Maybe.'

She gives me the small word gift, wrapped in hope, and I take it.

47

Every morning starts the same. Routine seems to help. I check my email to see what Riley has going on and reply. I try and limit myself to two or three emails before getting dressed but it isn't always easy, because he's always got so many funny stories about his dad's farm. And then there's the painful jokes. But I know that once I close down my laptop the panic will kick in – the fear that I'll forget to take my Fluoxetine. I start listing all the things that could happen if I forget to take the little green and yellow pill. I start to wonder what I'll do if I lose the box. And on it goes.

I've stared dicing the packets up, just in case. Some are in the bathroom cupboard for emergencies, a few are in my bag, which goes everywhere with me, and the other foil tray is next to the fruit tea Mum's bought me in the kitchen. It helps now I don't have to hide it from Mum and Nonno. I don't have to bury them underneath my bras and knickers. It's as normal as the fruit tea, *almost*.

'It's your audition next week isn't it?' Pryia asks as just as we're about to go into the ward.

'Yes.'

'How do you feel about it all?'

I shrug. Part of me is nervous in a normal way and another part of me feels calm and ready. I talked it all through with Nonno. He didn't say anything I hadn't heard before about what music means to me and to him. But this time, I believed him. It was the truth talking and I was able to hear it.

'I feel ready.'

'Good. You are. So, what are you singing for your contemporary choice?' Pryia asks.

'Nina Simone's "Feeling Good".' Just saying the song title out loud makes me feel happy. The trumpet and trombone make me feel bold, the flute makes me feel free and when all the saxophones come together I feel good. *Really good*.

We've got a big steam clean this afternoon. Every four weeks every single item Singing Medicine owns gets cleaned within an inch of its life. I won't see Pryia much after this week, apart from at the concert on Saturday night. We'll be at choir practice but it won't be quite the same. We won't be working together any more.

Nico throws a rattle on the floor as he sees us. Pryia passes him another but he throws that away as well.

'I give up. He just wants you.' She swaps places with me, moving to the end of Nico's cot. He claps his hands in delight. 'Little monkey! He's got what he wants!' She can't help but laugh at Nico's brazenness.

'Hop! Hop!' he shouts, reaching his chubby hands through the cot bars to me.

'Hope,' I tell him again, but he can't get the end right. Him I'm going to miss, but he's being discharged tomorrow anyway. We sing three songs to him before moving on and leaving him behind, calling out, 'Hop, Hop back.' But I can't. It isn't fair if we spend all the time with Nico, much as I might want to. I'm getting better at this, but I can't deal with another Kofi, not yet. I wave goodbye to Nico, ignoring his fake crying. He shows his back to me.

This isn't the only thing I'm getting better at, I realise, because my phone isn't in my pocket. It must be in my bag in my locker. It isn't surgically attached to me, resting in my palm like a security blanket. I won't be able to check it until lunchtime and that's fine. I can wait until then to read his latest email or to finalise our plans for Saturday night.

On Saturday night we'll meet again. It won't be like meeting a stranger because of everything we've shared. Last night we watched a really old movie together, *Sleepless in Seattle*, despite the sea between us. Our meeting place will be slightly less impressive than the top of the Empire State Building but Birmingham is doing its best by us.

'What did your mum say when you told her about the audition?' Pryia passes me another castanet. 'How did she take it?' she whispers, conscious that Mum is only across

271

the room, cleaning away.

'Better than I thought she would,' I admit. 'Actually, she was brilliant.'

'Did you tell her about me?' I know what she means instantly and I wish the answer was no, but I needed Pryia as back-up, as a case study of someone who not only has PMDD but is coping out there in the real world, functioning, someone Mum respects and trusts.

'Sorry,' I admit.

She shrugs. 'I would have too. Don't worry about it, it isn't like it's a secret. I'm fine with people knowing. So...' she presses.

'She got it. She understood,' I say, hoping that Mum does understand.

'Uh huh.' She waits for me to say more. So I do. I tell her about the conversation in the garden of remembrance, how Nonno came and found me in my room, after Mum had filled him in, and how he took my hand and told me all about Nonna and her problems.

'I never in my life thought I'd talk about periods with my grandfather, let alone hear about my grandmother's *menstrual misery,* as he called it,' I tell Pryia, pulling a face. 'I kind of wish I'd talked to him before,' I realise. 'I wish I'd talked to everyone sooner,' I admit.

'I told my dad before I told my mum,' she confides, 'it doesn't matter who you tell as long as you tell someone. It isn't safe to be on medication without someone knowing.

I was going to tell your mum if you weren't. Sorry.' She shrugs again and her sorry is too light and fluffy.

'Wow!' I'm speechless.

'I know what you're going to say but you'd have done the same,' she says, but I'm not convinced. There's no way Callie would have told my mum. No way.

Nonno sits on the back row. I can see him once I've cleaned my glasses. He takes his hat off and places it on the church pew next to him. He doesn't see me, but I watch him for a bit and this calms me down. Despite what I said to Riley, I am nervous. Just a little bit.

The church fills up – we've sold out. I keep looking and looking, searching the rows of people for him. I try and picture him on the ferry, his dark hair, his rich skin, his denim jacket, or was it leather? I can remember his lips and his grin, which was almost sly but just shy of it. But that's it. It's hardly a photofit but we decided not to send each other photos; it was too cheesy. I scan the faces in front of me and smile when I spot Callie and her parents – they must have got here really early to get such good seats. Ethan's there too, sitting on the end of the aisle just in case he needs to leave. Callie gives me a massive over-the-top thumbs up and I roll my eyes at her. She pokes her tongue out at me then puts her hands together as if she's going to pray. I snort but I'm so glad she's here. It makes me feel calmer.

'He'll be here, then you can tell him your good news,' someone whispers in my ear, making me jump. I turn in surprise and bump noses with Mum. My glasses fly off and the programmes she was carrying thud to the floor. She leaps forwards to catch the programmes and treads on my glasses. We hear the scrunch.

'*Oh no*! Hope, your glasses. I'm so sorry…' she starts.

'What are you doing, creeping up on me?'

We both reach down to the floor at the same time. She picks up my crumpled glasses.

'They're ruined,' she tells me pointlessly. Even with my limited eyesight I can see that. 'I've got a spare pair in my car, I think. They're in the glovebox, I'll go and get them.'

'We haven't got time. The car is parked too far. Never mind, it doesn't matter. I can see the sheet music fine. I can get them later,' I reassure her. I don't want to make her feel any worse. Owen gives her more programmes. She mouths sorry at me again as she walks to the back of the church to hand them out to people standing. There aren't any seats left.

I calm myself by searching for Nonno again. Even though he's blurry, I can make out his shape. I raise my hand to wave, but he's talking to someone. He's moving his hat to let the person sit next to him, already deep in conversation, his head bent. I can't see well enough to read his face anyway. I wonder if he'll hold up his hand.

'It's time to warm up,' Nikhil tells us.

I feel vulnerable without my glasses. We go back into the vestry for our last warm-ups. I'm a bit nervous now. I've never sung in public with this choir and even though I've rehearsed with them a few times, it's always different in front of an audience.

We climb up into the balcony, Mum close behind me in case I slip, and we light our candles. A hush falls over the congregation below. Mum and I make eye contact and for a split second it is as if we are the only ones in the church. The candlelight softens her deep-set brown eyes, highlighting her scattered freckles and the smile lines which are starting to creep back in around her mouth. Her whole face lifts when she smiles.

Owen starts our chant and he and Nikhil's baritones fill the eaves, until they're joined by Mum and the other sopranos, Pryia and the altos, and finally it's me, the only contralto in the choir. Together our voices flood the church with our blended sound.

We stand on the stage for our finale. The audience are invited to join in. Callie is one of the first to stand up. Her dad and Ethan are missing, probably outside. Callie hates hymns and churches with a passion but she's here for me.

The candle flickers as I open my mouth and sing my

first solo with the Singing Medicine choir. And it feels
good.

49

After the concert I stand in the street outside the church, waiting. I push my spare glasses up my nose, they really pinch. My face must have grown? Do faces grow? They definitely don't fit as well as my normal ones. The rain keeps on dripping and spitting in a half-hearted way. I wish again that glasses came with windscreen wipers. I swipe my jumper over them, which doesn't help. I check my phone to see if he's emailed or even called to cancel. I thought he might turn up when I walked back to the car for my glasses, so I ran, possibly not the best idea. Poor eyesight and rain aren't a winning combination.

There's a text. I knew it! He's not coming. It doesn't matter, it's fine. I open it. It's from Callie.

Turn around. See me in the window? I've said a prayer for you, you know how God and I like to hang, so everything will be fine, promise.

Have a little Hope (see what I did there?)
<3
Cx

'Hope?'

I recognise his voice instantly. I turn. He's got his leather jacket on again and fitted black jeans tucked into big boots. His hair is longer and darker than I remember and tied back off his face. He has a beauty spot right by his mouth, just one. He looks like he did on the ferry, but a bit softer, with fewer edges. And this time he's not smoking, so he smells a lot better.

'I did it,' he announces, instead of hi or hello or how are you.

'Did what?'

He's just whizzed forwards to what matters, like we do in our texts.

'I left.'

'Well, yeah, I can see that. You're here, aren't you.' Why is he stating the obvious?

'No, I mean really left. *Left.*'

'What? The farm?' I ask, getting it now.

'Yeah!' He grins, but I can tell he's nervous about it. 'I'm after seeing the world.'

'Really?' I didn't think he'd ever do it. 'Where are you going?'

'Everywhere. To all the places!' he says happily. We face

one another, his face lit by the street lamp, he's really smiling and I find myself mirroring him.

'You booked a ticket?' I feel the pleasure of it for him, his sense of achievement.

'*Yes*! I'm going to…' he starts, but I hold up my hand.

'Hang on a minute, Dublin. Are you telling me that you're not over here to see me? You're seriously saying I'm just a stop off on your great big adventure?'

I ruin the moment by grinning. He looks very relieved.

'Ah, here, I thought you were serious then. I mean I could have flown from anywhere, right? I didn't *have* to choose Birmingham Airport. Come on now, give me a break?' He pushes me gently. 'And I didn't come empty-handed. Oh no, Ms Caps Lock. I bought you something.' He rummages in his jacket pocket and pulls out a box. It looks like a jeweller's box.

'If you get down on one knee I'm out of here.'

The lining is blue with a bracelet sitting in the middle. I pick it out – a brown plaited leather band with a small silver link which has *be brave* engraved on it. Riley puts it around my wrist.

'Thank you, it's beautiful.' I look at it rather than him.

'Apparently these bracelets are all the rage with the PMDD crew or at least that's what the lads on the forum told me,' he says. 'I hope I've got the right one…' He tails off.

'What forum?' I'm lost. 'Which lads?'

'A PMDD one that I joined. Deadly serious now, I didn't know there were so many of you out there. And good woman yourself dealing with all that shite on your own until now,' he adds, looking at me like I'm some kind of wonder. 'I know you don't need it to remind you to be brave, you're already there, but I hope you like it?' He sounds so unsure of himself, so different in person.

'I love it. You really did it then, you really booked a ticket. And you told your dad? Please don't tell me you've run away?' I half joke and he gets it. He remembers what he said to me on the ferry.

'Everyone's a comedian. I told me da how I felt and it didn't go well, but he said he'd work something out, even gave me a wee bonus on top of my wages. Said it wasn't fair, like, to me. So I headed to the big city before he could change his mind. This is all because of you, y'know?' he adds quietly. We're stood very close to one another now.

'Because of me?' We're inches apart.

'Yeah, you, *Hope.*' I can hear his breathing in between his words. He says my name in a way that makes sense, in a language I'm fluent in.

'I heard you sing, in the church. I snuck in at the back,' he whispers, and I wonder why he's whispering. It's not as if there's anyone else out here.

'You did?' I whisper back.

'Yeah, I sat next to some old guy. He moved his hat so I could sit down and then started telling me all about his

281

granddaughter in the choir and how amazing she is. He said, "Wait until you hear her voice, you will have heard nothing like it," and then I knew who he was. Your Nonno!' He waves his hands around as if he orchestrated the whole thing.

'And?' I want more. I press the new bracelet against my skin.

'And he was right. I'll not lie to you now, you almost made me cry in there.'

'Oh,' I reply articulately.

'Yeah, *oh*,' he teases, moving in closer.

'Did Nonno realise who you are? Or did you tell him?' I want to know if they talked about *me*.

'Course. I introduced myself to your man, would have been rude not to,' he smiles. I wonder what Nonno thought of him. I want to know if he liked him.

'And?' I lean in to hear his answer.

Riley closes his eyes as he tries to remember Nonno's words. 'He said, "Good to meet you at last."'

'So, what happens now?' We're back to standing and staring.

'I guess we should talk about the thing we're both not talking about?'

I know exactly what he means.

'I got in, I passed my audition!' I manage to get the words past my massive smile. 'Is that what you meant, Birmingham Music College?' Maybe he was on about something else.

'I knew you'd do it, and after hearing you sing tonight, the lads in that music school would be mad to turn *you* down. You're all set then!' He reaches forward and hugs me like he's been waiting for the right moment. After what feels like quite a long time he pulls back. I look into his eyes – there's no sea between us now, nothing to divide us.

'So, are you going to email or text me from Canada? Or is it Australia? No, wait, don't tell me… *New Zealand*?'

'Harsh, Hope! But yeah, there might be a wee bit of truth in what you say.'

I fiddle with his bracelet, read the words again.

'And?'

'And what?'

'Do you want to carry on while I'm at music college and you're off on your travels?'

'Maybe. If you do?'

'Definitely. And you'll be coming back, not disappearing off the face of the earth again?'

'Maybe coming back. Definitely not disappearing. Scout's honour.'

'So, I'll call you then or email, whatever. Even better, how about a plan B?'

'Maybe, depends what your plan involves.'

'I'm doing a bit of travelling myself actually.'

'Are you, *actually*? Where you going then?'

'Italy. I'll be there for Christmas.'

'*Bueno.*'

'Yeah, except it's *bene.*'

'Anyway, tell me about this plan B.'

'Right, plan B. I was thinking, maybe we could meet up, in Italy?'

'You and me, Ms Caps Lock?'

'Yeah, *you and me*, Dublin! You know, if you want to, *maybe*?'

'Definitely.'

And although it's not quite the Empire State Building – and it's raining, and there isn't a gentle Hollywood breeze blowing through my hair – we stand together holding hands on a Saturday night on Charlotte Street.

Acknowledgements

I always read the acknowledgements first when I buy a book, I like to know about the team behind it because as we all know it does take a team, if not a whole village, to write a book. For *Hope*, I had a very BIG team so bear with me while I thank them all (brace yourself for a long list).

Firstly, thanks to my editor, Janet Thomas, who loved *Hope* from the start and understood the story I was trying to tell even when I didn't quite get it myself. Janet is one of those editors who sits quietly listening to me talk about my characters and then asks me one very intelligent and leading question. This question sends me off down a rabbit hole and when I emerge much later she's there, ready and waiting with another question. Diolch, Janet.

Secondly, thanks to my agent, Gillie Russell, who also loved *Hope* from the start and talked about my characters like they were real people. When Gillie talked about Nonno or Kofi I felt as if she really knew them and that made all the difference. Thank you for reading so many drafts of *Hope*, Gillie, and always responding as if it was the first time.

I had a talented team of early readers for *Hope* and I can't express in words how much it means to have had such passionate feedback and responses. Thanks to: Jo Nadin for falling in love with Riley – I so enjoyed your updates as you read; Katy Moran for your hawk-eye editorial skills and understanding of those hospital scenes & love for Nonno; Eve Ainsworth for excellent notes, completely and utterly getting *Hope* and all your help on shoutlines; Eloise Williams for your wise words of wisdom, constant support, humour and lifesaving daily chats; Joanna Courtney for your detailed feedback and encouragement; and Becca Kelly for your wonderful notes and meetings over coffee – Becca, you should have been an editor. And of course, last but not least, thanks to Helen Tracey (also known as Mum) who has read everything I've ever written and amazingly continues to do so, even when I use swear words.

Grazie molto to the PR wonder that is Megan Farr. Meg was my go-to-girl for all things Italian and I hope Luca didn't mind me borrowing his name.

Thank you to my publisher, Penny Thomas who has the power to say yes or no. Hopefully, (see what I did there) she'll continue to say yes.

When I applied for an Arts Council Grant for *Hope,* I didn't think I'd get it. It sounded too good to be true but when that brown envelope arrived with those magical words (and the all-important offer of money) it gave me the courage and the faith to write this book which at times has been challenging. Thanks to Zoe Marriott for talking me through the complicated process, I'd never have done it without you. The year I spent writing full-time was one of the best of my life and I'm eternally grateful to the Arts Council (and Zoe) for making *Hope* happen.

When Guy and Eloise Manning (the artistic dream team) told me their vision for the cover of *Hope* I almost swooned – they described the very first picture I had of *Hope* in my head, before I'd even written the first line of the opening scene. Guy did such a wonderful job with *The Boy who Drew the Future*, I knew *Hope* was in the best of hands. Thank you both for all your support, you disgustingly talented couple.

Thanks to Rebecca Ledgard, Singing Medicine™ Co-creator (with Sally Spencer) and Director of Education for Ex Cathedra for meeting with me one rainy morning in Birmingham to tell me all about how Singing Medicine came to be. Singing Medicine is part of Ex Cathedra's education and participation programme. Thanks to the whole Singing Medicine team and Birmingham Children's Hospital for inviting me to follow you round the hospital with my notebook and pen and many questions. The biggest thanks of all goes to the patients of BCH who let me sing with them and the nurses who were very nice when I got in their way.

Singing Medicine is a registered trademark and can only be delivered by Ex Cathedra's Singing Medicine team. http://excathedra.co.uk/education-particaption/singing-medicine

I'd also like to give a big shout out to Readathon. Last year they gave over 25,000 new books and provided 210 storytelling days in hospitals, bringing the magic of books and stories to over 100,000 seriously ill children and their families.

readforgood.org

I'd like to thank all my students for being so supportive of my books but special thanks go to Asia Khan and Fatima Patas for our many conversations about hijabs, Muslim culture and children's literature. Your detailed answers to my many questions are much appreciated as is your enthusiasm for *Hope*. I'm so proud to be Bordesley Green Girls School's Patron of Reading and I'd like to say a big hello to the students and staff and a massive thank you for being so excited about *Hope*.

Kate Taylor, you were very helpful with your local knowledge and love for Shrewsbury. Thank you for telling me about The Bird's Nest Café.

Rachel Lucas and Dawn Jones, you both gave me invaluable (and honest!) advice and insights into autism, travelling with an autistic child and the education system. Thank you for letting me borrow the social stories book idea, Dawn, and for sharing Otis's with me. I hope I have got it right with Ethan, any mistakes are of course my own.

I really don't know where I'd be without my YA writing group, you help in every way imaginable, making me laugh, improving my shoutlines and keeping me calm on a daily basis. Big hugs to Keris Stainton who let me use her gorgeous book *Starring Kitty* in *Hope*. If you haven't already read it, *go,* what are you waiting for?

Whenever I've had a problem in my life I've turned to books, fiction and non-fiction alike to show me the right path or at least point me in the direction of a new one. I was so pleased to see http://reading-well.org.uk/ set up Books on Prescription, if *Hope* helps just one reader with any of the issues covered then I'm happy.

Thanks to all my readers and friends on social media who have been so supportive about *Hope*.

Kisses and cwtches to my family (sorry, Evie for accidentally calling you Hope) for putting up with someone who lives half in the real world and half in a made up one. The best world is the one with you all in it x

Ex Cathedra:
Ex Cathedra is a leading UK choir and Early Music ensemble with a repertoire that reaches from the 12th to the 21st centuries. They are known for their passion for seeking out the best, the unfamiliar and the unexpected in the choral repertoire and for giving dynamic performances underpinned by detailed research. Founded in 1969 by Jeffrey Skidmore OBE, the group has grown into a unique musical resource, comprising specialist chamber choir, vocal Consort, period-instrument orchestra and a thriving education and participation programme, aiming to explore, research and commission the finest choral music and to set the highest standards for excellence in performance and training. Singing Medicine™ is Ex Cathedra's award-winning project for children in hospital.

Author's Note

PMDD Support groups and advice:

NAPS – http://www.pms.org.uk/

PMDD awareness UK –
https://www.facebook.com/pmddawarenessuk/ Gia
Allemande Foundation –
https://giaallemandfoundation.org/

GURL – http://www.gurl.com/2014/11/06/pmdd-
information-facts-treatment-for-teen-girls/ TEEN PMDD
– http://teenpmdd.weebly.com/

break the cycle 2017 PMDD Annual Conference October
4 – 6, 2017 www.giaallemanfoundation.org

Further reading available on the *Hope* page at the Firefly
website www.fireflypress.co.uk